Praise for Gregory Miller and his books:

"Gregory Miller is a fresh new talent with a great future."
—Ray Bradbury

"Miller's prose has a luminous clarity rarely seen in a postmodern age where mysterious opacity is often touted as a virtue...He addresses the reader in a poetic language that is translucent, heartfelt, and wise."
—Roderick Clark, Editor of *Rosebud Magazine*

"The small town life depicted in *The Uncanny Valley* is in many ways familiar and comfortable territory, but each story demonstrates that something unnatural lurks beneath the surface. As the stories coalesce to form a larger narrative, the perversity builds...On its own, each individual anecdote is merely curious; as a collective, they become morbidly sinister."
—*Booksellers Without Borders*

"Miller's intriguing premise and incredibly creative stories had me completely enthralled...One of the best eerie books I've read."
—*Book Matters*, reviewing *The Uncanny Valley*.

"[*The Uncanny Valley*] is an inspired and original idea, breathing fresh life into a popular and revered genre."
—Novelist and critic Daniel Cann

"Gregory Miller's tales in *Scaring the Crows* are wonderfully dark, wonderfully various, and wonderfully wrought."
—Brad Strickland, award-winning author of the *Grimoire* series.

"*Scaring the Crows* is a delightful collection. The stories are chock full of heart and description, and you're left amazed that you could grow so attached to the quirky and often quite likeable characters in such bite-sized works."
　　—*Hawleyville Reviews*

"It's easy to imagine [*Scaring the Crows*] being done by one of the old greats…This book is a treat."
　　—*Book Reviews Weekly*

"Miller's prose is unique in that it's both straightforward and elegant. The combination makes the stories powerful regardless of their length and ensures that the endings, one of the author's fortes, have an impact on readers. The range of subject matter in this collection is only matched by the skill with which the author blends nostalgia, humor and the uncanny."
　　—*Buzzy Mag*, reviewing *On the Edge of Twilight*

This book is for Samuel and Andrew

"I can believe anything provided it is incredible."

--Oscar Wilde

Table of Contents

Prologue

In June 2009, WRDB, a Central-Pennsylvania NPR affiliate, launched a narrative project as part of a "small-town cultural preservation campaign," asking listeners to address, in 2000 or fewer words, the following prompt:

> Describe a specific event—historical, ritualistic, or personal—that typifies the culture of your hometown.

From the submissions, ten finalists would be chosen. The authors would be contacted, receive a small cash prize, and be invited to read and record their pieces for on-air broadcast. Anthology publication was also a possibility.

Within two months the station received over 12,000 essays via mail, email, sound file, or video. Judges for the contest, including four WRDB employees and a well-known "special-guest" essayist (a local newspaper columnist), noted that a significant number of submissions, thirty-three in all, came from the same location: Uncanny Valley, a small town apparently located in the south-western part of the state.

Typical responses from most essayists described autumn festivals, Christmas pageants, veteran parades, acts of kindness, local heroes, and other benign traditions, events, or people. Some (generally the exception) focused on the dark side of their respective local cultures: racism, violence, greed, hypocrisy.

The submissions from Uncanny Valley, however, addressed a quite different angle of small-town living...

What follows are the thirty-three submissions from Uncanny Valley received by WRDB. They have been reproduced exactly as submitted; in the interest of accurate documentation, spelling and punctuation have not been corrected. The order of the submissions is loosely based on the order in which they were received. It should be noted that all arrived via standard mail, none contained return addresses other than "Uncanny Valley, PA," and all were either handwritten or composed on manual typewriters.

A number of conclusions may be drawn from these submissions. Admittedly, a hoax is quite likely. Yet the unusual nature of the pieces, in terms of both content and circumstance, warrants, in this humble compiler's opinion, a more thorough investigation than has yet been undertaken. Further research will hopefully shed light on what remains, at the moment, a very singular event.

TITLE: "The White Dove"
AUTHOR: Norton Weiss
AGE: 79
OCCUPATION: History Teacher, Uncanny Area High School (retired)

Mr. Robert MacDowell was one of the saddest people in Uncanny Valley. No one doubted that.

It wasn't that any dramatic tragedy had befallen him. No deaths of children or massive injuries. No house burning down or financial collapse. No, no, Robert MacDowell had simply been worn down by life, dulled by routine...Oh, what the hell. It was his wife who made him that way. It was Gertrude.

She was a force of nature; a nasty combination of dominance, selfishness, and manipulative prowess. A genius for getting what she wanted. All of his friends saw this and loathed what she did to Robert over the years, but none of us could do a damn thing about it. Bob was hooked, trapped, ensnared...you supply the term. He was obviously miserable, but a spell had fallen over him, and during the worst of Gertrude's behavior—a tantrum at Bernie Oldman's funeral; an affair with Jack Grenny, the worst postman in Uncanny Valley's history; a thrown catheter bag at What's Cookin' at Casey's—he'd just looked sheepish, flashed a goofy smile, shrugged his shoulders...

You get the point.

Well, last year the happy couple's Golden Wedding Anniversary finally rolled around. For me it was a long half-century, although I don't have much else to compare it to, and I'm sure it was especially long for Bob. For quite a while, deep down, all us old cronies sensed there was some kind of dark animal lurking behind Bob's passive ways, but by then what friends he had left had seriously begun to doubt it was still prowling around. The man was old, getting frail, had recently lost a lot of weight and looked fish-belly pale most of the time. He didn't have long to live, that much was certain. It broke my heart to see him.

For three years, Gertrude had been planning a vow renewal ceremony to mark the occasion. Bob would mention it now and again—how she wanted everything *exactly* as it had been fifty years ago when they exchanged their vows in her parents' back yard.

Not so much to ask, you might say, but when Gertrude said "everything," she meant *everything*, and when she said "exactly," she meant *exactly*. She poured over old photographs and journals and scrapbooks, looked at fabric swatches and paper samples and linens, viewed the old guestbook, and invited every last person who was still alive—not many, but a few—then added to it as she saw fit. And Bob, of course, was the lackey who had to take her to all the stores scattered across the countryside, who had to purchase everything, who had to listen to the incessant revisions and daydreams of the perfect day—*her* perfect day—as it had been in her memory and would be again, if she had her way.

But the kicker was the house. Gertrude's parents' house had sat abandoned for over two decades, and damned if she didn't make Bob buy the dump and have it all fixed up. That way, she said, they could have the reception inside, just like the first time. "How *special* it will be!" she exclaimed. "How *beautiful!*"

Gertrude's father, the town blacksmith, had hated Bob since Day One: too puny, too *bookish*, he'd constantly reminded everyone. Her mother, all 400 pounds of her, had quivered with rage whenever Gertrude registered a complaint about Bob—which had been often. They both died in bed at the same time, thanks to a carbon monoxide leak early one winter morning. Once, in a rare (perhaps lucid) moment,

Bob told me, "If that leak was a man, I'd have bought him a drink."

Finally the day arrived—a fine July day full of humidity and mosquitoes (bred in the rain barrel Gertrude had forced Bob to buy for the sake of "Old Times"). An expensive white gazebo stood newly-erected in the freshly seeded and mown back yard. The cake was carried to its table on a square wooden slat by half a dozen teenagers. The minister tottered in and began to mingle, shaking hands and nodding distractedly. Gertrude had invited practically the whole town, and practically the whole town came. (No one, despite their ambivalent relationship with Gertrude MacDowell, wanted to miss *this*—not after the catheter bag incident.)

The only concession to change that Gertie allowed was fans—three high, pendulous electric fans on poles that would, most of us felt, save her the indignity of collapsing from the heat…or of saddle-bagging her satin sleeves, at the very least.

Well, things got rolling at high noon. There was Bob, standing on the white gazebo step with a faint, tired smile on his wan face. There was Reverend Beckman, ninety-two years old and likely not quite certain where he was. There were the geriatric bridesmaids, the sixty-year-old ring bearer, and the audience, all two hundred of us, restive and ready.

And then, finally, Dolly Carlton blasted out the Wedding March on her windy old organ and Gertie proceeded down the aisle, led by her corpulent son Desmond, her face aglow in too much makeup, her ill-fitting chipmunk dentures gleaming.

I glanced at Bob. He looked unsteady on his feet. His hand, wiping at his brow, shook noticeably. But he kept smiling; smiling for his wife who was never pleased, who always wanted something more or something different.

But amazingly, perhaps miraculously, the smile faltered when Gertie, taking her spot beside him, whispered too loudly, "Really, Robert, you're sweating through your suit… and with the fans running, too! You're *embarrassing me!*"

Yes, indeed, the smile faltered. And when it returned, damned if it wasn't grim.

That was all it took; we had witnessed the final straw alighting on the camel's back, and the camel's back had broken. Something, after half a *century*, had finally snapped in Bob. The dark animal had woken up.

I looked around to see if anyone else had noticed. Carl Fuller had; he was clasping his hands and leaning forward expectantly. So was Roger Burlington. And half a dozen others, too.

Finally, Reverend Beckman's thin, reedy voice declared, "Now Gertrude and Robert will release a white dove to symbolize their love, two spirits as one until death do them part."

Oh, Christ, the dove. The last, great crisis of the whole project. Where to get a white dove? There *had* to be a white dove, just like before, because that was the *symbol*, that was the *climax!* It *wouldn't be a good ceremony without a white dove!* And so Bob had traveled to nine different pet stores before finding one in central Ohio that stocked white doves. All to make Gertie happy.

And she was. I could tell. She was *very* happy. *Ecstatic.* This was *her moment.*

Gertie reached into the cage and removed the dove, cursing as it scratched her with a tiny talon, then handed it forward so Bob could take hold, too.

By now, everyone seemed to have noticed Bob's expression. A murmur ran through the crowd. They *sensed* something was coming. *Felt* it. Bob cupped his hands around the bird. Gertie held the legs.

"Ready?" Gertie breathed.

"Allow me," murmured Bob.

With a surprising burst of speed and strength, he jerked the bird away, took it in one hand, then *heaved* it up into the air like a baseball...

Straight into the back of the nearest electric fan.

It exploded like a watermelon hitting concrete. A fine, red mist rained down on the crowd, followed moments later by a lazy sprinkle of blood-flecked white feathers.

"Home run!" Roger hollered out, and then we were all on our feet, Gertie's friends and family screaming in horror, Bob's friends cheering with sudden, unexpected pride. And Bob, a wide smile on his face, the happiest I'd seen him since we were kids, sauntered away from the gazebo just as Gertie, face contorted, white dress sprayed scarlet, fell with a crash off the steps and died of shock on the spot.

Bob walked on home through the crowd with confident strides, a champion in chaos, feathers still drifting down around him. He died of cancer two months later, but that doesn't matter; those last two months were *good*.

And I swear, leaning toward me but not looking in my direction as he passed me by, Bob murmured, "Till death do us part."

TITLE: "In Tune"
AUTHOR: Diana Gerts
AGE: 54
PROFESSION: Grocery Clerk

People have been curious about Eugenia Wentworth since I was a little girl, so I figure it's time to set the record straight. After all, each and every day for fifty years she's worked at Wentworth's Grocery, adding up tabs, filling orders, weighing ham and cheese on the counter scale, keeping the coffee pots warm, stoking the fire or cleaning the fans...you name it. And for thirty of those years, I've worked alongside her.

She owns the place now. Her pop, old Eugene Wentworth, he's the one who opened the store way back when, and he finally got called home to the Lord some eighteen years past. Died out back, unloading crates of string beans. So the store is the legacy he left her. That, and a few other things.

Old Eugene was a talker. Knew everyone in Uncanny, since they all came in now and again. He had the only general store in twenty miles. And if you ever wanted dirt on someone, he had dirt to give. He could make a man's ears burn a thousand miles away. He could make the dead wince.

But Eugenia, she wasn't a talker. Still isn't. Instead, she used to sing.

She had a beautiful voice. Everybody thought so. Even in grade school, from what I hear, though she's a good ten years older than me. I heard her sing once when I was a little girl—some high school musical or other. I remember her black hair and her white dress, but especially her voice. She didn't just sing music. Her voice *was* music, if you get my drift. It was a fine voice…light and airy and full enough to make the skin crawl in a strange, good way.

But her father didn't care about that. Distracted her from work, he said. He never showed up to hear her in church or at town functions. He never gave her a word of encouragement. And as she got older she ended up black and blue more than a couple times. He wanted her in the store, and that was that. Her good talents distracted people from *him*, and it was *his* world that mattered, not hers.

It wasn't until she turned sixteen that she tried leaving town. She had a horse hitched up, bags packed, a new hat for New York City in a twine-tied box and twenty-seven dollars in her reticule. She aimed to make it big, and to heck with her pop, and to heck with his store, and to heck with Uncanny and its tiny goings-on! She was heading off, and no one was going to stop her.

What brought about this decision is common enough. There was a man…some quiet romance blooming in the late summer evenings. He encouraged her to leave, said he'd go with her, that they'd start fresh in a bright, new place.

But the very thing Eugenia and her beau were trying to escape is what did them in: the great wheel of small-town life and the gossip that keeps it turning. Old Wentworth found out.

Just as she was saddling her horse, convinced her pop was fast asleep, Eugenia heard a noise, turned, and there he was, face pale and quivering with rage.

"Who is he?" Wentworth demanded. "Who *dares?*"

But she wouldn't tell. Wentworth kept at it, whipping himself up into a towering fury, but still she kept quiet.

So that's when he pulled out the straight razor.

I can imagine it, although I don't want to: the old man forcing Eugenia to the ground, prying her mouth open, dipping the blade in, down, and across her tongue, his voice mocking, screaming, as *she* screamed through the blood and all her dreams fell to dust.

After that night, Eugenia wasn't seen for months. Then one day she appeared, pale and silent, behind the checkout counter. And she's been there ever since.

That much the gossip tells. But one day I stumbled across a tatty little notebook in the storage closet filled with writing in Eugenia's hand, and that's not all there is to the story. Nope! That flimsy old notebook was chock *full* of this and that, and even though I only caught a quick glance (and the notebook has since disappeared), that was enough.

Wentworth died out back by the loading gate, that much everyone knows. They also know he was murdered "by a person or persons unknown"—someone took a straight razor and slashed his throat clean across. What they don't know is that he, too, had been relieved of something important to him: his ears. Those big old ears that took in all the town's talk before his tongue could add to it and send it back out again. Old Sheriff Nelson must have kept that quiet. Discretion was something of a strong point with him.

As was a sense of justice.

What's left to say? That's *my* gossip, and it feels good to get it off my chest. Oh, and only after Wentworth died did Eugenia perk up and begin to hum. These days everyone likes to hear it. She hums so pretty, so well. And she's always in tune.

TITLE: "The Fourth Floor"
AUTHOR: Gary Hughes
AGE: 19
OCCUPATION: Mechanic

We moved to Uncanny Valley when I was ten. Pop said he never intended it. We was driving through town on our way to Pittsburgh for Aunt May's funeral, and everyone seemed taken by it after we pulled off the overgrown exit and had lunch at What's Cookin' At Casey's. I guess that happens a lot, if you bother listening to the old men down at Wentworth's. They say it's a hard place to find and a harder place to leave. And sure enough, next thing you know we'd picked up and moved from Pottsville, rented a cottage, and settled in. And here we are still. It's a pretty good town, I guess—a little small, but the people is mostly pleasant (and the girls mostly good-looking). And there's lots of nooks to poke around in, for all its size. It's not dull, I mean. Yeah, that's for sure.

Well, it took three years for my folks to save up enough to quit renting and buy the house on Pugh Street. It was worth the wait, though: a big old fixer-upper dating back to the 1840s, four stories high, eight bedrooms, and an attic cupola on top of it all. A real mess, but my folks and me and my older brothers started cleaning it up real quick. All of us is good with our hands.

To save money on heat, when fall rolled around Ma and Pop shut off the top two floors of the house. All the cash went into getting the first two floors on the up-and-up. By October Pop had the whole downstairs re-floored and re-plastered, new wiring and ductwork up and running, and an indoor bathroom built from scratch that worked just fine.

He also built new kitchen cabinets and bought a stainless steel sink.

By the beginning of November the second floor was in pretty good shape, too. We'd been sleeping in the parlor in roll-outs before that, but Pop got the walls and windows and ducts finished, though not the floors, so the three bedrooms on the second floor was at least ready to sleep in come Thanksgiving.

That's when the noise started. On the second floor we could hear it clear, me and my brothers, every night: a thumping, always the same, like a clock ticking but too loud, or maybe a water pipe clanking when it got full of air.

It would start around midnight, after most of us was asleep, and sometimes my brothers slept through it from start to finish. But I was a light sleeper, and it bothered me to no end, and it kept up for a good two hours every time, and I hated how constant it always was—never changing, *THUD... THUD... THUD*, until I thought I'd go crazy.

I never liked bothering Ma and Pop with such things, but it got to the point where I was always tired in the morning and that wasn't no picnic. It'd have to stop.

So one morning early in December I said something about it over breakfast. Pop asked some questions, and Gerald and Tom said they'd heard it, too.

It seemed an easy enough topic for morning talk, and probably an easy enough thing to fix, but we was all a bit taken aback when Pop turned to Ma and said, "Mona, you ever hear that at night?"

And Ma said, "No, can't say as I have."

And they gave each other strange glances, like they knew more than they was saying. And that didn't make sense to me, because it was such a small thing. Anyway, how could they not hear it?

So Tom said, "Well, mind if we unlock the stairwell to the third floor and take a look, Pop? We've all heard it and it's keeping Gary up all the time. And he's bothersome when he's cranky."

But Pop said, real quick and fierce, which is unlike him, "You'll do no such thing, kiddo. I'll take a look later on. But I won't have you on the upper floors when they ain't safe yet. You read me?"

And that was that, at least for a time.

*****

When you put your head to the heat vent in my bedroom, you can hear down to the living room. It's like playing telephone with two cans and a string. Well, the way my folks'd looked at each other when I brought up the noise at breakfast had me curious. So that same night I crept out of bed and put my ear down real close in case they talked about it. And sure enough they did.

Pop said, "We can't have the boys scared, can we, Mona?"

And Ma said, "No, we've got to find a way to keep them out of there. Don't know how we'll do it when it comes time to remodel that floor, though."

"You sure you don't mind it? That you aren't afraid?"

Ma kept quiet for awhile. Then she said, "It's unpleasant to have around. But this is a nice house and we can't let a thing like that send us away. Live and let live, I say. And if it keeps on thumping around we'll just wear ear plugs, that's all."

And Pop grunted, then they both fell silent.

Well, like any kid who has his hackles up about something and isn't supposed to do nothing about it, I did something about it. I creaked open my brothers' bedroom door and gave them both a nudge, and after they got done cussing at me, I told them what Ma and Pop'd said. And they both got real quiet, and that's when the thumping started up again. It was midnight.

So Gerald, he said, "OK, Gary, we'll have a look tomorrow night. Ma and Pop will be out at the fire hall dance real late."

And that was that. We'd see what was what.

The next night, right about midnight, Gerald pulled out a rusty skeleton key and fit it in the lock of the old oak door to the third floor staircase, turned it, and pushed the door open real slow.

A wash of cold air hit us from above. I flicked on my torch and we started up the scarred wooden steps.

There was two more bedrooms and what Ma called a "sewing room" and some closets and such up there. All the wallpaper was falling off the walls and there was broken old furniture scattered about. But we couldn't find nothing to explain the noise.

Then it started again, which is what we'd been waiting for.

We all froze, listening good. "It's coming from above," Tom said softly.

I looked at him. "You ever been up there?"

"Nope," he said. "But I bet the door to the stairs ain't locked. Come on."

I followed behind him and Gerald. They opened a worm-eaten door and we clumped up a spiral staircase, the wood all springy from rot.

"Careful," Gerald said.

The fourth floor was dark as pitch and close with dust. There was three more rooms up there. The first was full of old newspapers and smelled like mold. The second had baby dolls on the floor without no heads and bits of other toys, too. But the sound wasn't coming from either.

"It's a damn shutter flapping, I bet," said Gerald, stumping over to the doorway of the last bedroom. The sound was sure coming from inside. It was real loud now.

With a snort, he kicked open the door.

I never heard someone scream so loud as he did when he shone his light in there. Tom looked in and yelled, too, and that was it. They raced out, stumbled down the hall, and slammed back down the stairs. But I had to look, of course. So I stepped up and shone my light into that room. And what I saw was a woman in a tattered old dress, walking into the wall in the back of the room, thumping and thumping, over and over, and the sound was her head hitting the plaster. And when I gasped, she turned a little toward me, and I saw why she kept bumping into it. She hadn't no eyes, just empty black sockets. And she smiled real wide, too wide, and her teeth was too big, and that's when I ran. I ran and ran and screamed and screamed and when I got downstairs it took both my brothers a long time to calm me down, talking to me and patting me on the back and hugging me tight and telling me I'd be OK.

We wondered if she would follow us down, but nothing showed. And after a long, long time, Gerald made himself go back up and shut the door to that room. When we asked, he said she was still in there, but hadn't turned his way...just kept bumping and bumping against the wall, like before. And then he locked the door to the third floor good and tight.

Well, Ma and Pop was pretty angry with us when they got home, but they also felt mighty sorry we'd had a fright. They'd seen the ghost a while back but kept quiet for fear of scaring us. And none of us ever figured out what the story was behind it, but we decided to stay anyway. It was a nice house, after all.

And when we fixed up the top two floors, Pop left that one bedroom alone and locked it up real good and tight. And the ghost is still in there most nights, but we all got ear plugs, so that fixed that.

26

TITLE: Our Halloween
AUTHOR: Lily Travern
AGE: 51
OCCUPATION: President, Uncanny Valley Ladies'
Aid Society

Every autumn Farmer Gill begins tending his pumpkin patch. All the rest of the year it's pretty much left to its own to do what it will, but when the pumpkins begin to grow, he has to see to them, turning them, pruning, prepping. Then, always the beginning of the third week in October, he sets up his little lean-to stand by the street and fills it with pumpkins. He hires neighborhood boys to help pick them and move them to the road, until by the end of the second day there's piles and piles of pumpkins spreading out in big hills all in and around the stand, set amongst bales of hay. And he sells cider and gourds and Indian corn and apples, too. Goodness, but those apples make fine pies!

Farmer Gill loves Halloween like all get out, and he has a special thing he does with pumpkins—a trick, you might say. Because of this he gives people two choices: they can buy their pumpkins early and carve them up personally, or they can wait until the morning of October 31ˢᵗ and buy them then. About half his money is made before Halloween and half on the day itself.

Why, you might well ask, do so many people wait?

Well, sometime between the tolling of the midnight bell and six a.m. on Halloween morning, every one of his remaining pumpkins—hundreds and hundreds, piles and piles— become jack o' lanterns, each perfectly carved with faces and animals and words and scenes and sayings. And all lit, too! So, when the citizenry who don't care to carve their own all gather in the frosty pre-dawn Halloween morning, they find a ghoulish tapestry of orange and yellow light glowing and flickering from the most extraordinary display you're ever likely to see.

And then out comes Farmer Gill from his little stand, chipper and smiling and freshly-shaven, his straw hat cocked on his head, a black cat pin fastened to his overalls.

"Well!" he says every year. "Looks like there's still plenty to choose from, folks, all ready-made by my dear friends. Step right up and take your pick! Fifty cents each and that's a bargain."

No one knows who his "dear friends" are. No one has ever admitted to helping him out, and the pumpkins are the same pumpkins that were sitting out there uncarved the night before. People have checked. Every once in a while someone goes up and asks him how he does it, hundreds and hundreds in one night, and he always replies, "Well, if you love Halloween enough, there's folks who know it and lend a hand. Now go choose!"

And they do, and my, but the town does look good on Halloween night!

TITLE: "By Moonlight"
AUTHOR: Jeffrey Turner
AGE: 16

In winter, I guess two years ago, me and some friends was staying over at Paul's house. Paul's was always a good place to go because his parents never cared what we did. Then he moved away last year and things aren't so much fun now.

But this time, it was the Friday of the start of Christmas Break, and there was four of us, all fourteen: Kirk and me and Dan and Paul. Paul's parents had gone I don't know where, and that was fine by him and the rest of us. And we all went to spend the night at his house.

That night was a good time. We watched a bunch of movies downtown, then went sledding out by the construction site until we got too cold, then we came back in and made hotdogs and told scary stories. Around midnight we got bored doing that, and no one wanted to be the first one to go to sleep, so we started thinking up something else to do.

It was Dan who came up with the idea of going out to look for the hut in the middle of the pine woods. There aren't no pines in the forest around Uncanny except in one place: a cut between roads about three miles long. In the center there's this old hut made of stone, and sometimes we found bottles of beer inside that weren't all finished. So we decided to go see what was what over there.

It was real cold by then. We put on our coats and scarves and gloves and headed out. We didn't need no lights because the moon was so bright, and it wasn't snowing anymore even though it had been falling hard all day.

We'd been going along for a fair pace when some storm clouds covered the moon and the snow came on again. Suddenly the night got real dark, and since we was already in the forest a bit, it was kind of hard figuring out where we was going or how far we needed to get before we found the hut.

But after a long time we got there. There's stories about that place, of ghosts and other sorts of nonsense. But I don't believe none of that. But even without any ghosts we got scared that time. We got scared real good.

The snow fell thicker as we got close. It landed on our hats and in the catches of our scarves. It was real cold that winter. But even through the snow, the moon came out again all sudden-like. It had been too dark to see more than shapes in the night, but now everything was all pale and silver. And it was then we saw the deer.

It was like a garden of them. It was like they'd growed right out of the ground. But they was all dead. Four dozen, maybe five, all laid out still and cold in the overgrown field around the cabin. They looked like they'd just laid down to rest, maybe catch some sleep. But their eyes was all open and shining like crystal in the moonlight. Besides, we all knew they wasn't sleeping. Deer don't ever sleep.

Well, my daddy told me once how there's times when a body just *knows* something's wrong. Sometimes that feeling comes when you can't even see nothing, you just know. But we saw plenty, and we knew things weren't right. There wasn't a mark on those deer. No bullet wounds, for starters. And none of the bloat or tongue biting from poison. They was more deer than we'd ever seen in those woods in all our years put together, and all unaccountable dead.

Paul took off first, followed by Kirk and me, then Dan. Dan, some think he's brave, but I know he's just stupid. It takes him longer to figure things out, so he didn't figure out to start running until the rest of us was long on our way out of that place. But of course he came too, once his thick head turned the idea around that we hadn't no business there.

And that's almost it. I guess just that would be enough, but there's a little more. The next night we went back again, this time just after dark so it wasn't so lonesome. We wanted another look. Kirk didn't come, but Paul and Dan and I went back. A fresh six inches of snow covered the ground, and it was still real cold, so there shouldn't of been much change to them bodies. But when we reached the hut and fished around a bit in the clearing, all that was left was skeletons. No fur, no skin or muscle. In one day those deer went from perfect to skeletons. And that was enough for me. I never went back.

But like I said, Dan, he's a bit of a slow one, so one day come spring he thought he'd go back there again. Paul went with him, just to make sure he could get the true dirt. And when they reached the clearing where the hut should have been, there wasn't no deer, and there wasn't no hut, neither.

And when I tried to go back to that place to see if *they* was fibbing, I didn't find no clearing.

TITLE: "What Happened to Charlie"
AUTHOR: Bernie Thompson
AGE: 10

Mr. Upton down near the dam owned a tiger. A real honesttogoodness tiger. He bought it from a karnival that aimed to kill it and took it home and gave it good food and started showing it off in the barn for two bits a look.

One day Mr. Upton took Charlie (thats the tigers name) out for exersise and Charlie got loose and run off. So for three weeks after Charlie came on into town and farms at night and kilt off a bunch of dogs and cats and goats and sheep and chickens and even one of Mrs. Deeners cows.

Soon they got a party together to go hunt for Charlie. Uncle Jack was with them. Mr. Upton was pretty upset cause he wanted Charlie alive and he also was pretty upset cause he had to pay for all the dead pets and livestok. But no one would here any of it from him so they set off into the woods with riffles and traps.

They didnt catch Charlie and they didnt even see him. Charlie was a clever tiger. He wouldnt let himself get cought. For three days they looked for Charlie. Then one day they saw a bunch of crows and vultures cirkling a spot in the woods. They headed over their real quick to see what was what and what do you think they found but Charlie, but he was dead and there wasnt a drop of blood in his body, only a bunch of little holes all thru his skin. And their was a big bite out of him too that was bigger then a bear could make. And their was a tooth left behind but I never saw it. Uncle Jack says it was like nothing anyone he new had ever seen. I know cause I herd him talking to Grandpa when they didnt think I was listning.

After that they kept us kids away from that bit of woods. But none of us wanted to go their anyway after the story got out.

Grandpa says Uncanny Valley is a thin place. I dont know what that means except what happened to Charlie sure must have something to do with it. I guess thin places is more fun than most. They keep us on are toes.

TITLE: "Richard Shute Goes Home for Dinner"
AUTHOR: Carl Fuller
AGE: 81
PROFESSION: Proprietor, Fuller's Gas Station

"I'm thinking about going home for dinner tonight."
"Sure you are, Richard. Sure."
"Right, Richard. Have a nice meal, will ya?"
The old men outside Wentworth's Grocery moved chess pieces slowly across scarred boards, half in thought, half in reverie. One of them (me) said, "How you going to find your way, Richard?"
"How do you think? I lived there fifty-five years! You going dense on me, Carl?"
I shook my head, sipped some coffee from a wax cup, and took Roger Burlington's rook.
"Shit on you, old man," snarled Burlington.
"I'm two years younger than you, King Tut," I replied, and everyone chuckled.
"But I *am*, though," continued Richard.
"Richard," said Norton Weiss, tapping the sidewalk impatiently with his cane, "you keep going on about this every damn day. You sound like a broken record."
"I'm just declaring my intentions, is all."
"Well, stop it. Or go home for dinner and be done with it! I hate a man who declares his intentions then doesn't follow through." He knocked pipe ash into the rain barrel.
"You don't think I can go home?" For several minutes Richard had sported a far-away look, but now he seemed sharp again.
"What, two doors down?" Weiss scoffed. "I'd hope so."

"That's not what I mean, and you know it." Richard took Weiss's knight with his bishop and knocked it clean off the table. "Check mate, damn it."

"This all started a month ago," I said. "What's eating you, Richard? At first you were doing fine after the move."

"Well, I'm not now. I'm damned sick of how things are. And soon, maybe not today or tomorrow, but soon, I'm going home for supper. A real good supper. And that's God's honest truth."

He stood up abruptly, swayed on his feet so I thought one of us would have to catch him, then started slowly off down the street.

"Hey, we're not finished here!" Weiss called out.

"You're beat and you know it," Richard called back.

"And you're going the wrong direction!" I said.

"It's the *right* way, damn it, the *right* way."

We watched as Richard tottered off into the haze of the early autumn sunset. Then Burlington looked us over with sad, hard eyes and said, "Someone ought to call his son, let him know how the old man's behaving."

"Richard Shute hasn't talked to his son in seven years," I said in a low voice. "It isn't proper for us to meddle in that."

"Carl, the fellow isn't *right*," Weiss interjected. "The screws in his brain are getting rusted out. We've all seen it happen before, and it's clear as crystal that's what's happening now. Like it or not, Richard's in a bad way. Christ, just the other day I saw him standing at the edge of Seney Street, looking down toward Lower Uncanny and talking to himself."

"Well...that's not a good sign, I'll give you that," I said slowly. "Should I catch up and herd him back in the right direction?"

"Nah," said Burlington. "Not this time. He'll walk around the block and find his way back eventually. Always has so far. But soon, now. Soon..."

And he left that word hanging there for all of us to consider.

*****

Less than a week later, I was walking home in the first cool of the evening, admiring the changing leaves on the maples and oaks, when I came across Richard sitting on the same bench where Norton had spotted him. That far-away look was deeply etched in his face, and his cheeks were stained with drying tears.

I sat down beside him, heart beating hard. He was a very old, good friend and seeing such behavior hurts like hell. The man *never* cried. And now, too, he was talking to himself again.

"Coming," he whispered. "Real soon. I hear you."

I followed his gaze. Before us, down a steep incline, was all that was left of Lower Uncanny.

"Richard?" I said gently. Then again, louder.

He started, looked around with wide eyes, saw my face, and his own crumpled. "Oh, it's only you," he said.

"Who were you expecting?" I asked.

"Never mind."

"Richard...what's the *problem?*"

He sighed. "This isn't where I belong."

I opened my mouth, but he cut me off.

"Look at me, Carl. Son grown. Daughter dead. Wife dead. My old house taken away. Bad ticker. Bad memory. The play's over, the house lights are up, the audience is gone, but I'm still on the damned stage. I want to go home too, and not to that stifling little one-room apartment on Main Street, neither."

I sighed. "You ever read Thomas Wolfe, Richard?"

"Can't say as I have."

"That man knew what's what. He wrote, 'You can't go home again.' And I'd say he's mostly right."

"Well, that's all well and good for Mr. Wolfe, but I intend to try," said Richard. "And I got some help, too."

I didn't like that one bit. A shiver went up my spine, like something was prancing about on my grave.

"What do you mean, Richard?"

"I mean," my old friend said (and his eyes looked very clear when he said it), "that I'm going back to my *real* home. Soon. And I aim to stay there this time."

I looked out toward the remains of Lower Uncanny—at the wide, flat expanse: a burial ground in its own way.

And it was then that I decided Burlington was right. Richard's son would have to be called. Right away.

We said our "goodbyes" in the fading light, and I remember wondering if I would ever see him again.

Call it intuition, or just common sense, but I didn't.

He disappeared that same night.

*****

A little boy named James Rice was the only witness. Jimmy claimed he saw Richard right at nightfall, maybe half an hour or so after I left him. He was picking his way down the incline toward the water's edge, murmuring. Jimmy thought that was funny, so he called out, "Hey, Mr. Shute, whatcha doin'? Fishing?"

According to Jimmy, Richard replied, simply, "Proving Thomas Wolfe wrong."

And then he slipped beneath the waves of Uncanny Lake and disappeared.

You see, Lower Uncanny lies beneath fifty feet of water; has ever since they finished the new dam. Eight dozen houses buried in a vast, deep lake.

Divers found Richard some weeks later floating in the dining room of his old house, way down under all that water. They went in through a blown-out window, looked about with a light, and there he was. No one could figure out how he got himself down there; Richard couldn't swim for shit.

And floating nearby, adrift by the ceiling, was another body, obviously dead far longer. And it took some work, but the sheriff's department determined it was Susan, Richard's wife. Only problem was, she'd been buried in the cemetery over by Uncanny Hill three years before. But when Bill Dixon dug up the grave, the coffin was all clawed up on the inside, broken, and empty.

TITLE: "The Great Unknown"
AUTHOR: Jeremy Lochran
AGE: 22
OCCUPATION: Coal Miner/College Student

Above Arcadia Street, behind the great back yards of the richest families, the woods rise, dip, rise again, give way to fields, then regroup and plummet down with the land into a deep gorge where no one I know has ever gone. But as children we went as far as the dip between the rises, following a narrow stone path that started on the other side of the stream at the edge of old Mr. Donald's property.

Without exaggeration, I haven't thought of that path more than half a dozen times in twice as many years. Nor of the pool at the end of it.

Until today.

The pool. We all knew it and we all saw it. The overgrown path goes on a long way, several miles, and the woods are thick, so it's not a place for casual visiting. But yes, every child I knew went there at least once.

For me, it was *just* once. I went with Eleanor Doverspike and Jack Sproul, a few days after the July 4th of my ninth year.

The older kids had been talking it up, so we got bit by the bug and had to see it too. And Eleanor and Jack were my closest friends, so there was no question but that we'd go together.

Once we'd decided to make the hike, we had to undertake some preparations. We each needed a bottle. We each needed something gold. And we each needed a thin slip of paper.

Well, paper was everywhere, and even getting the gold was easy, at least for me. I just pried a link off Mother's necklace one morning while she was taking a bath. She never noticed it was gone. But it took time to find the right bottle. Only a pale-blue glass bottle would do, and those had gone out of fashion, so I ransacked the attics and sheds of every family member I could think of until I found one—a castor oil bottle Grandpa Davis kept fish hooks in, but which he no longer needed, seeing as how he'd died the previous winter.

No one knew why only pale-blue glass bottles worked, but that's what we'd been told, and we wanted to do everything right. Eleanor found her bottle a day later, and Jack already had one set aside, so once that step was out of the way, we weren't held back any longer. We scratched our initials in them with a pin, and made ready.

We left early in the morning, just an hour after sunrise. For children, it was a long hike, but the presence of the other two kept each of us determined; alone, I doubt any of us would have made it the whole way.

My memories of the path are vague now. I remember we carefully checked to make sure Mr. Donald wasn't looking, then slipped along his side yard, ran down through the overgrown brambles of his back garden, and jumped the stream to find its start. Beyond that, I have a hazy recollection of flat stones, summer heat, milkweed pods, and golden sunlight shifting through green leaves…and how long the hike seemed—*very* long—though now, I'm sure, it wouldn't seem like much. That's all.

But the pool? Even now, my memory of the pool is sharp, focused, and fresh. I don't know how that can be, but it is.

The stone path ended in a small clearing circled by woods, and in the clearing grew tall, rustling wheat. And beyond the wheat was the pool, ringed by a carpet of soft, green moss—except at the far end, where a tall outcropping of rock overshadowed the deepest part, and the waters flowed softly beneath it to be swallowed by darkness. The rest of the pool was shallow, bathed in sunlight, and crystal clear, fed by an inexhaustible spring deep in the earth.

We stopped and sat on the mossy bank, feeling it beneath our hands as we took it all in.

"Look at all the bottles," Eleanor breathed, pointing. "So many."

They were everywhere, floating on the surface of the water, placed carefully on and around the rock outcropping, and lining the mossy bank. Each light-blue glass. Each stoppered with a cork or sealing wax. Each initialed. Some few had broken, or lost their seals, and lay on the sandy bottom of the pool, glittering through the refractive water.

And while we sat there, staring, there's no other word for what we felt but enchantment. We were in a special place, a magic place. We were about to join something great, something mysterious, something old and strange and beyond all of us.

It sounds ridiculous to write about it, or would have before today. But that pool is a wishing pool. We called it that, or "Wishing Waters," "Glass Lake," "Mermaid's Home"…there were—are—so many names for it.

Then we stood back up and went to work. We got out our bottles, our gold, and our papers. We also got out a needle, passed it around, and pricked each of our index fingers. In blood, we wrote our wishes on the little slips, then carefully scrolled them up and slid them into the bottles.

We knew better than to ask each other what we'd wished. If we told, the wishes wouldn't come true. So we corked the bottles in silence and found places for them. Eleanor chose to leave hers standing on the big rock. Jack left his floating in the water…I remember him casting it off from the shore like a toy sailboat, and how it bobbed toward the center of the pool. And after long thought, I placed mine on a little bank of wet pebbles, where the water lapped gently at the shore if the wind blew. I figured she might see it there.

Jack then fished around in his pocket and took out a gold earring, I withdrew my mother's chain link from a folded handkerchief, and Eleanor removed a slim gold wristlet from a little purse.

"Ready?" Jack said.

We nodded.

"Mermaid of the pool, take these three gifts for our three wishes. Make them come true, we ask of you." Then he cleared his throat and added, "Thank you." He looked embarrassed. We were too young for formal speeches, but we knew the words had to be said.

Then we threw our payment into the deep water by the rock outcropping, where the gold would be taken by the current into the cave, then far underground, to the depths where the mermaid was said to live.

Yes, a mermaid. On the surface, a silly fantasy cooked up by children with too much time on their hands and over-active imaginations. Yet we took her very seriously, for the stories were deeply ingrained: how once a year she emerged from the deep underground waters and chose one bottle. How the owner of that bottle had his wish granted, provided he'd prepared everything correctly. And how tampering with another child's bottle, even slightly, could get you killed, if she took notice. She was fickle, and dangerous, and power-ful—or so we believed.

I remember, as we turned to go, looking back at that quiet, sun-drenched glade, and at the pool, the hundreds of bottles in and around it sparkling in the hot sunshine, and feeling certain—*certain*—she was real.

And then we left.

And it astounds me now, how quickly memories can fade.

For several more years I wondered if my dream would come true. But as more time passed I grew disillusioned when I thought about my bottle, so carefully prepared, so that I didn't mention it to anyone anymore; I felt foolish, like I'd left a note to Santa Claus that might someday be found and used against me.

Then that feeling also faded, and I stopped thinking about the place altogether.

Until today.

I'm 22 years old. Tomorrow morning I'm set to catch a lift to Plumville, and from there the train to Pittsburgh, where I'll begin my classes to become an English teacher. It took five years' hard work in the Sagamore mines to save up enough, and half a dozen scholarship applications, but I finally scraped together the money for tuition and got the acceptance. Not many Uncanny High graduates are so fortunate, and I'm grateful that, at long last, I may have a chance to start a career, rather than work in danger my whole life the way my father and grandfather did.

So it's been a busy and emotional day, full of "goodbyes" and promises to write, squaring accounts both professional and personal, packing and preparing.

Two hours ago, exhausted, with the sun setting and my whole body screaming for sleep, I trudged up the steps to the second floor of my old house, my parents still chatting quietly down below, and lay down on my old, familiar bed, surrounded by suitcases.

And it was then that I happened to glance up at my little writing desk, and saw it.

My bottle.

It glimmered in the darkening room like a fading star. It *still* does. And when I picked it up and realized what it was, tracing those old, scratched initials with a fingernail, all the memories of that long-ago day came flooding back...and with them, that extraordinary sense of wonder; that belief that *anything* might be possible; the indescribable sense that a Great Unknown still existed in the world that was beyond my comprehension.

I noted that my cork was still in the bottle, but the contents of the bottle had changed. My message, my little slip of paper written on with my own blood, was gone.

Shaking, I pried out the cork with my penknife and slid out a thin sheet of light-green parchment. And as I unrolled it, I remembered my wish, so carefully stored away for so many years:

I wish I could meet you.

And there, now, on that strange, beautiful paper, in glowing silver letters, was the simple response:

Come to my home at sunset tomorrow.
Your wish will be granted.

Sunset tomorrow.

At sunset tomorrow, I have the chance to make my childhood dream come true. I could walk the old stone path, come to the clearing that so often filled my dreams as a boy, wait in the darkening evening, and see something I only imagined ever seeing…and never thought I would.

Or I can be unpacking in my new apartment, meeting my roommates, getting ready for my first day of college.

For two hours, now, I have weighed my options. Even while writing this, I have continued to weigh them. But now the answer is clear.

The sense of wonder…the belief that *anything* might be possible…the indescribable sense of a Great Unknown…

It never left. It only changed, as I have.

College it is.

I can hardly wait.

TITLE: "My Flower"
AUTHOR: Rachel Gregor
AGE: 14

I've had Flower since I was born. He's always been with me. My very own dog.

Ever since I can remember he's sat at the foot of my bed by night and walked at my side by day, even to school.

Especially to school. And back, of course. And he even sits by my desk while Mrs. Wilson teaches English and Mr. Burton teaches math.

Of course no one can see him but me. That's part of the family curse. According to Mom, he came with us from England when the Gregors moved to America in 1877.

But I don't know what sort of curse it is to have a dog like Flower around. He never hurts anyone in the family. And he's great for when kids pick on me.

Take Jason Peters. Every day, starting in first grade, he had it out for me. He stole my hat, took my candy, pushed my head in the snow and knocked me into puddles. At first I did what Mom and Dad told me to do. They said to be polite and not sink to his level. So for almost a year I did that. Sometimes Jason got bored picking on me and left me alone. Sometimes he didn't. But I got used to him, even though I didn't like it.

Then, early in third grade, Jason got worse. I came home crying. My parents got worried. And Flower started growling when he saw him.

I tried to stop Flower. All I had to do was put my hand on his head like Mom told me. That calmed him down.

But then, the day of my seventh birthday, Jason went too far. I had on my new dress, one Mom made for me herself. It was beautiful. And while I was walking to school holding a tin full of cupcakes for my class, he came up behind me and pushed me into the biggest, deepest mud puddle I ever saw. My feet flew out from under me and I fell all the way in on my face.

I remember him laughing, and how my dress was all ruined, and thinking how the kids wouldn't get any cupcakes now. And then Flower started growling. And I looked up at Jason, and then at Flower, and just nodded my head.

And Flower sprang up and ripped out Jason's throat.

The police never solved the killing. No one else was there to see it except Mrs. Wallace, the old crossing guard lady, but she's half-blind and was too far away.

Some time later Mom and Dad sat me down and told me how disappointed they were. They said I knew better, that I'd been warned what would happen if Flower got mad.

That's when I asked Mom about Flower's past.

All she said was, "The locals in England used to call him Black Shuck. He's very old."

"Older than Grandpa?" I asked.

"Much older. And he's a cursed creature. He's been with our family many, many generations."

Some people think I'm crazy for talking to an imaginary dog, so I've learned not to speak to Flower when others are around. But I know he's not imaginary. So do my parents. And from the look on Jason's face right before he died, he knew it, too.

Sure, Flower may be a curse.

But not to me.

TITLE: "Mrs. Karswell's Garden"
AUTHOR: Edith Schretengoss
AGE: 56
OCCUPATION: Nurse

For years, Mrs. Kaswell's garden was the most beautiful place in Uncanny Valley. Everyone thought so.

She lived in a big, three-story Victorian at the end of Arcadia Street. The walkway up to her front door was all steps—49 of them—and her back yard was just as steep, with a thin, finely manicured grass path leading down through the living contours of trees, bushes, plants, flowers, and moss to a smooth, slow-running brook she kept lined with white stones.

All the children used to visit her, me and all my friends and practically everyone I knew, because her garden felt like a safe place, a special place, and no one ever intruded there who didn't belong. If one of us had a problem and needed a think, we'd run to the goldfish grotto by the violets and stay there until we figured things out. If one of us got beaten by our parents or made fun of at school, we'd hightail it over to the cascading birdbaths and watch the falling water and the flitting birds until our breathing slowed.

Often Mrs. Karswell herself would be there too, watching the birds—sparrows and doves and robins and bluebirds and cardinals and finches and who knows how many other kinds. She was an old woman, some said the oldest in Uncanny (though I've heard different), and even the grownups said they had never known her when she was young.

My clearest memories of her are the purple dress she always wore, the silver hair she kept tied back in a bun, the wrinkles around her light green eyes when she smiled, and her kindness. That, most of all. She didn't talk much, but she listened very well to our little crises, gave us cookies and lemonade, and always made it clear that the white picket gate to the back garden, heavy with Morning Glory vines and flowers, was always unlocked for us, and we were always welcome.

I had a daddy who drank too much and liked to knock me and my big brother around, so Danny and I were often over at Mrs. Karswell's and got to know all the secret nooks and crannies of the garden very well: the hidden statues, the silent spring that flowed into a tiny pool covered with white lilies hidden under the lilac bushes, the butterfly tree...I could go on and on.

So perhaps that's why she talked with us a little more than she did most children. And perhaps that's why she sat us down on wicker seats in the white gazebo near the little creek one August afternoon and told us her secret worry.

"Children," she said, "I hate to burden you."

"Anything, Mrs. Karswell," Danny said. He was eleven. I was nine. He was a quiet boy, a bit fragile, but always shoveled her steps when it snowed during the dark winter months. He showed his affection in gestures, not words.

Mrs. Karswell smiled and cleared her throat. She'd been doing that a great deal over the previous few months, and had also caught a nasty cough somewhere.

"Children, you love this garden very much."

"Sure we do, Mrs. Karswell," I said. "Sure!"

"Well, it's going to need some help. I have to leave, and I need someone who can take care of it for me."

Danny and I stared at each other, shocked. "But... why do you have to leave?"

Mrs. Karswell smiled again, her eyes bright. "Because there comes a time when everything has to be passed along," she said simply. "So I want to give it to you. Would you like to have it?"

I don't remember what I said. Probably my jaw just worked a little. But Danny said, "You mean, like a gift?"

"That's it!" Mrs. Karswell slapped her knee. "It's a gift."

"But how would we take *care* of it? We don't know how to garden."

"Everyone who comes here will help out. That's the way it's always been. I've never so much as touched a spade in my life! All you have to do is keep it safe, and it will do just fine."

She turned up her palms, and, I swear, they *glowed*.

Then, with a gentle motion, she took Danny's right hand in her right hand, and my left hand in her left hand, and squeezed them tight. At first my hand just tingled, but then it grew warm, pleasantly warm, and it felt as though soft currents of water were pulsing up my arm...

Finally, sighing, she let go. The glow in her palms had disappeared, but the warmth remained in mine. And Danny's.

"Now it's yours," she said simply, then coughed long and hard.

Shortly thereafter, we said "goodbye" to Mrs. Karswell and headed back home. She looked tired—exhausted—and we didn't want to wear her out. We asked no more questions.

And we never saw her again.

*****

Mrs. Karswell died two weeks later, and after that, every time we went near the property *our* hands glowed, just like hers. Sometimes, late at night, they shone like dim stars.

For several months we visited the garden every day. And our friends came, too. And so did others, lots of others, and the garden thrived, even as summer turned to autumn. Mrs. Karswell's birds landed on our shoulders and ate from our hands. Leaves fell like gold and crimson flower petals and floated in the current over the white stones. In winter everything faded, hibernated, slept beneath the earth, but in spring we came back again and the garden blossomed as beautifully as ever.

But then there came the practical business of a property deed. Mrs. Karswell had also taken care of that, but legally the house and grounds belonged to our parents. We were too young. For six months they talked about what to do with the property, and there was even some discussion of moving in. But Daddy, he was a thoughtless man, and even as early May saw the lilacs bloom he drew us together around the dining room table and told us Mrs. Karswell's house would be put up for sale. "That money," he said, "will come in awful handy."

A man named Mr. Donald bought it. He didn't much care for gardens and he didn't much care for children. And when he moved in, our hands stopped glowing because we weren't allowed near the garden any more. I cried and cried, and even Danny wept when he thought no one was looking, but there was nothing we could do.

One day in mid-summer, after Daddy went on a binge and beat us both for something small, Danny and I decided to *sneak* in. We missed our thinking spot by the spring beneath the lilacs and we missed the warmth of our glowing hands.

But when we got there, all we could do was fall to our knees and stare.

All the trees were gray. All the flowers and ferns and plants lay like corpses, brown and rotting. Muck clogged the spring. And by the dry birdbaths lay the fragile skeletons of six-dozen birds.

Then I noticed my hands. They were cold. So, so cold.

Mr. Donald saw us from his window, ran outside, and shooed us off the property with a cudgel.

That was the day my childhood ended.

TITLE: "Keeping Dry"
AUTHOR: Jenny Sumpkin
AGE: 12

My mama told me a story one time she swears is true. She swears it up and down. But I don't know about that.

She said there once lived a man named Ben Sparks, right here in town a long time ago, and he was really scared of water. I mean he hated it. He took sponge baths, that's how bad he hated it. I guess he was scared of it because of something bad that happened to him when he was little. Mama calls that a "complex."

Well, finally Ben Sparks grew old and died. They buried him in Uncanny Cemetery and that was that for a long time. But many years later there was this big flood. We learned about it in class. It happened in 1897 or something like that. Definitely before World War I. A lot of town got swamped or swept away.

They figured that might happen someday. The town elders, I mean. They weren't very prepared, but they still figured it might happen. So even though lots of houses went, the cemetery was safe and secure. None of the coffins in the lower part floated up even though they were under ten feet of water. Big stone slabs held them tight.

Except for Ben Sparks. He was the only one who came up out of the ground. They found his rotted body snug and dry in the upper branches of a fifty-foot oak tree, way above the flood.

And after that they buried him on Uncanny Hill.

TITLE: "Here and There"
AUTHOR: Karl Godwin
AGE: 32
OCCUPATION: Contractor

Mr. Jarvis was my seventh grade teacher. One of his big hobbies was photography, and even though he taught Social Studies he was pretty famous for his photos. Every summer he put on shows of his work all across the country. He was also really big in France.

One day in late October Mr. Jarvis came in to class and something wasn't right. We weren't sure exactly what, only that something about him was different. Off.

Well, right in the middle of a lecture about the Battle of the Somme he stopped, and he kind of looked around all funny, and then he said, "Do you want to hear a story?"

And we all said sure.

And this is what he told us, as best I can remember.

*****

One time there was a man who liked to take photographs. His work was fairly well known and he made a fair amount of money, and every year he tried to complete a new series of photos on a new subject.

Well, one year his photographic study required some shots of old, broken-down machinery. He was trying to capture scenes in which nature was re-taking human habitation, and figured that machinery on a farm would be perfect, especially if the machinery was all rusted-out and the farm was abandoned. So he asked some friends if they knew of any abandoned farms that might work. And one of them told him about a place way out in the countryside, I mean *way* out in the countryside, far down a dirt road in some scrub fields all going wild again. It was old and long empty.

It sounded perfect.

He went out after finishing up his day job, right as dusk was settling down across the sky. It was late-October and growing cold, with dead leaves falling all around and wood smoke in the air. He figured an abandoned farmhouse out in the country would be very atmospheric at that time of the year and at that time of day, and he was right.

The outside of the farmhouse was falling to pieces. Some pillars like the kind on old plantations were leaning down at strange angles, and the bricks of the outside walls were covered with moss and lichen. The yard was all dry dirt and all the land beyond it was overgrown and tangled up in corn gone wild, so high he couldn't see over it.

The barn had burned, so no machinery was there, but up against the sagging porch he found a grain thresher leaning against an antique tractor all rusting to pieces. A big hornet's nest filled the front seat. That worked great, so he took plenty of shots and was quite happy with himself. And then he noticed the front door of the house was standing open.

Well, ladies and gentlemen, the photographer couldn't help himself. It was getting dark and he didn't have a flashlight and he was all by himself way out in the middle of nowhere and he hadn't told anyone where he was going…but he went inside.

It was worse than outside. Big strips of mildewed wallpaper had sloughed off the walls. The carpets were rotten and the floorboards warped. Bits of ceiling plaster, black with mold, drooped down like rotting leaves.

There wasn't a whole lot else to see, except for some piles of soggy newspapers and a broken roll-top desk. And the staircase up to the second floor, of course. That was hard to miss, because termites had gone to work and the whole oaken structure—banisters, stairs, and paneling—had crashed down in a heap at the far end of the room.

The photographer was disappointed. He wanted to explore a little, and now the second floor was out of reach. He checked the doors to some of the other rooms on the ground floor, but they were all locked.

Except for one.

A short hallway led to the dilapidated kitchen, and a door set in the left side opened smoothly outward as he pulled. Beyond, instead of a room, was a staircase descending down into deep and utter blackness.

The photographer paused. He thought a moment. He was alone, in a condemned farmhouse, and the sun was setting toward a cold, moonless October night. No one knew where he was. The steps might collapse under his weight. *Anything* could be down there.

So guess what he did? He started on down, of course. His curiosity got the better of him. He couldn't help himself.

Seven steps, and the light disappeared. The stairs held firm, but he couldn't see a thing. Even the idiot photographer knew he couldn't go fumbling around in the dark. Then a thought occurred to him: he could use his flash. Every five seconds or so he could take a picture and see what was there and where he was going. He had a bunch of bulbs in his pocket. That would do.

He continued down. Eventually his shoes touched packed earth. The darkness was like something you could cut, like a dense tapestry of spider webs.

He snapped a photo. The flash blasted the cavernous room with light before leaving him blinking and blind again. In the one second of illumination he saw a variety of jumbled trash—broken chairs, water-stained piles of linen, a mounted deer head falling silently to pieces.

Still blind, he stumbled toward it. Although not technically machinery, the junk would still make a perfect subject for his new portfolio. He removed the flash bulb and replaced it. He took another photo. Then another. Finally, one more.

Now, with full night fallen outside, the photographer turned to go. He was cold and damp. And the basement smelled funny, like mold and fungus and wormwood and…

And something *else*.

He sniffed the air. The basement was totally still, totally silent. The stench hit him again.

Something dead was down there with him. Something rotting.

He should have fled, but that's not what happened. Just like he shouldn't have gone to the house, just like he shouldn't have gone *in* the house, just like he shouldn't have stepped down into the basement, the photographer shouldn't have moved farther on into that deeper darkness, trying to find the source of the smell.

But he couldn't help himself.

The basement stretched behind the stairs, so he picked his way over to the junk, touched the stump of an overturned chair, and took another photo, this time carefully aiming toward the back of the cellar.

Against the wall, something lay slumped—a bloated, dark shadow. He saw it, his flesh now damp and cool…and continued forward.

Flash and step, step and flash, he moved on until he was standing before it, over it, gagging and choking at the stench.

He paused, exhaling out his nostrils once, twice…

Blindly, he kicked out at the darkness. His foot connected with something soft, something slick, something *yielding*.

And that something slid sideways to flop against the ground with a wet, heavy thud.

Hands shaking, he took a final photo.

The flash exploded, washing the basement with light.

A face stared up at him, eyes sunken in gaping sockets, lips curled back, skin green, fat, white worms writhing in its cheeks.

The photographer's scream echoed in the cavernous cellar and out of the house. He turned. He ran. He slammed into the stacks of trash and fell, righted himself, fell again, hit his head, and somehow found the stairs.

Up the stairs and down the hall. Down the hall and out the door. Out the door and to the car. In the car and to the sheriff.

An hour later he sat in the station, nervously bending a bottle cap.

"Sheriff Cobb'll be back soon," Deputy Glover told him. "You're lucky he don't fine you for trespassin'."

"I know I shouldn't have gone there," said the photographer. "I know it."

But four hours later Sheriff Cobb hadn't returned. Finally, a call came through. Glover looked irritated, then concerned. After hanging up, he told the photographer, "You go on home now. We'll call you in the morning."

"Did he...did he find the body?"

"Go on home now," Glover repeated.

The next day the photographer opened his front door to find Sheriff Cobb himself standing on the porch. The photographer made him some coffee and they sat down in the living room. Both men looked uncomfortable. Finally, Sheriff Cobb said, "Tell me something."

"Of course," the photographer replied.

"You said the body was in the basement."

"Yes."

"And your camera film at the station can prove it."

"All you have to do is have it developed."

Sheriff Cobb grunted and stroked his whiskers.

"You...you *did* find a body," the photographer said.

"Yes, we found a body," Sheriff Cobb replied slowly. "But…" He cleared his throat. "It wasn't in the basement."

The photographer's suddenly cold, suddenly damp hands clenched, unclenched, clenched again. "I don't un—"

"We found it stuffed in a closet on the second floor," Cobb finished. "Pretty far gone, but an obvious gunshot wound to the chest."

The photographer stared at him aghast.

"That leaves only one official possibility," said Sheriff Cobb. "If you didn't do this, and I don't think you did, then someone was in the basement with you, watching you, and—"

"No more." The photographer felt faint. "Please."

Sheriff Cobb set down his cup and stood to go. He tipped his hat. "Stay close," he said. "We may need to question you further. We still haven't got a name for the body and there's always follow-up when foul play's involved."

Just as Sheriff Cobb's hand reached for the doorknob the photographer grabbed his sleeve. He couldn't help himself.

"Wait."

The big man turned.

"Sheriff, *there were no stairs up to the second floor.*"

Cobb sighed, then nodded. "Yeah. We had to have Deputy Glover's hound dog pick up the scent. Then we got some ladders. That's the one thing that don't fit. We just can't understand it." He snorted. "You want the *un*official possibility as I see it?"

The photographer nodded.

"Either someone moves damned quickly and leaves no footprints, no ladder marks, no scent in the basement, and no tissue residue…or, well, I guess that dead fella *really* wanted to be found. Can I give you some advice?"

Numb, the photographer nodded again.

"Stay out of abandoned houses for awhile," he said shortly, then trudged back to his car.

*****

Mr. Jarvis finally fell silent. Everyone in class was staring at him.

Then he smiled. It was a strange smile.

"Anyone want a camera?" he said, and giggled.

I guess he couldn't help himself.

TITLE: "Coming Around"
AUTHOR: Maxwell Creevy
AGE: 36
OCCUPATION: Electrician

I'm not old, but after work I still like to snort around with the grumps at Wentworth's a couple times a week. They knew my grandpa, so they're like family...great-uncles, I guess. So that gave me plenty of chances to see Travis Walton in action.

Travis Walton never once knew when to keep his mouth shut, and that's a shame, since little that spilled out of it ever benefited anyone. He wasn't a nice fellow. Even into his fifties he wasn't beyond smacking a cue stick over a man's back after a late night at Schooner's, and he couldn't keep married since he beat every woman he got close to—either with his words, or his hands, or both.

Afternoons outside Wentworth's, he sometimes chawed with us before heading over to Schooner's, but we often had enough of him before long and told him so, especially when he started going on about colored folk. He had a deep streak of hate for them, though I doubt he'd seen more than a dozen his whole life, and hadn't spoken to one.

Mind you, the dislike we feel toward such talk isn't universal in Uncanny. Some people keep their prejudice deep and their mouths shut. Some few others *don't* keep quiet, and there's been a couple displays of such feelings over the years—all anonymous. But neither kind are as casual and loud as Travis was, namely because they know which way popular opinion goes on the subject, and that when the wind blows in your face, it don't do to spit.

Travis, he never learned that.

None of us could ever figure him out when it came to colored folk—or the Chinese, foreigners, Jews, or Baptists, for that matter—except that most of his family was mean going back a long way. And then there was his frustration over losing every job he ever had due to his own bad habits. A person who suffers from his own bad habits is almost never likely to blame himself. Everyone else becomes a target. And the folks who are different become the biggest target.

Travis lived on a large farm out beyond Uncanny Hill. The farmhouse was a hundred and fifty years old if a day, built by his great-great-grandfather, and there the Walton dynasties had come and gone. It was a large enough place, rambling and good-timbered, but he'd let it go to seed a bit. He still had the land, though. Lots of it.

One day Travis came into Wentworth's cussing up a gale. Eugenia gave him a look that would stop a weak man's heart, but he ignored it and slammed a twenty-spot down on the counter.

"I need a maul, two bags of cement mix, and a new lantern," he said, then turned to us. "Hell you looking at?"

Old Norton Weiss chewed on his pipe. "A rhino in a china shop," he said calmly. "A baby in need of a bottle."

"Shut your mouth, you goddamn book queer," he sneered. But even as he said it, Travis was tramping over to an empty chair by the stove.

"My hole of a basement flooded out worse than ever," he said, running a beefy hand across his sweating forehead then holding his palms out to the warmth.

"Melting snow," said Carl Fuller. "There's still lots more to come."

"No shit. Anyway, I fixed on the source and found a walled-up doorway at the far end of the fruit cellar. Most of the water was seeping from there. Never noticed it before."

Eugenia's heavy-lifter, Harry Ward, came out from the back storeroom and set a new maul by two big bags of cement. Eugenia clunked a lamp down beside them and rapped on the counter.

"Feels off," said Travis, lofting the maul. "Chink-made?" He scanned the handle. "Goddamn, but it is. Ain't you got nothin' else?"

She didn't, so he took it and the other stuff, still muttering, and slammed the door behind him.

*****

Only a few days later, we noticed something strange. Something that was damn-near a miracle, in fact.

Travis Walton stopped talking.

He kept coming by, but he drank a lot more coffee and said a whole lot less. He didn't take much interest in any of us, which was fine...just unusual.

Eventually word trickled in, courtesy of the gossip lines. He'd found a tunnel behind that bricked-up doorway in his fruit cellar, and a room at the end of it.

Worse: there were bits of candle stub in the room, and rusted-out lanterns, and a few rotting wooden boxes, and mildewed blankets and straw. Nothing too horrible for Travis in that, but under one of the blankets was a scratched-up old tin-type photograph: a tiny portrait of a colored man. This treasured relic had been left behind, no doubt, on a trek to Canada by someone on the run.

Yep. That's right. The buzz around Uncanny was that Travis Walton had stumbled across an old stop on the Underground Railroad...this one *literally* underground. Built, no doubt, by his own great-great-grandpa.

*****

It took the smallest of things to make him snap. He was waiting to erupt, anyone could see it, but Norton Weiss (God bless him) never did mind crossing the line with people he didn't like.

Two weeks had passed since the discovery. In the meantime, Travis had taken on something of a hunted look—what some might have said was only *defensive*, but it went beyond that. He was embarrassed, he was outraged...and he was *scared*.

The rumor mill had it there were things going on in the man's head that suggested insanity. Carl Fuller had it on good authority Travis was hearing voices in the house—whispers, mostly, but also crying and laughing—all coming from the basement. And Harry, who almost never interjected, stopped lifting grain in the back long enough to join us for a cigarette and add, "I was passin' out beyond the property late one night. Travis was settin' on the porch all by himself, but talkin' as if someone was there with him. 'You get gone,' he said. 'I'd kill you. I would at that! I'd hog tie you and flay you *deader* than dead. You just get, you just...' And so on. I didn't say hello, 'cause he sure as sugar wasn't talkin' to me. But you bet I picked up my pace until I was down the road a ways."

Shortly thereafter, Travis slammed in, eyes wide and bloodshot. His hand trembled as he slumped by the stove and lit a cig. None of us said a thing...except Norton, who relished his obvious discomfort.

"You know, Travis," he said in his most pleasant tone, "they say there's talk of putting a state-funded historical marker out by your mailbox."

"What? How's that?" The big man's tone suggested danger.

"Well, being as how your ancestor was an abolitionist, and being as how your house played a part in that particular historical movement, it stands to reason—"

Travis was up in a shot and straining for the old man's throat before we had the presence of mind to restrain him. He left the store raving.

*****

There remains little to tell. Actually there's a great deal left to tell, but it won't take long, because there's not much any of us can add to it by way of explanation. Just conjecture, and that's not worth your time.

Late that same night, someone broke into the cemetery and knocked Travis Walton's great-great-grandfather's headstone all to pieces. Shattered it to smithereens. Pissed on it, too. Sheriff Cobb said the damage was done with a heavy, blunt object.

The next day, early in the afternoon, Sheriff Cobb paid a visit to the Walton homestead. He found Travis's new maul, all covered in rock dust, lying on the front porch.

Travis was more difficult to find, but eventually Cobb turned him up.

He was in a tiny, dark room at the end of a dank passage that opened off the basement. He'd been hogtied, shirtless, over a rotting barrel, his back flayed to the bone.

It was blood loss that killed him. That and shock, more than likely. And that's all anyone ever could say.

TITLE: "Mittens' Last Catch"
AUTHOR: Mrs. Emily Winthrop
AGE: 63
OCCUPATION: Seamstress

I had a cat when I was little and her name was Mittens. I loved her very much. She was a calico, a tiny little thing.

One day Mittens went ratting in our barn. She was very good at catching rats, and she always brought them back to the house and left them on the door mat—usually one a week, give or take.

Well, late that day my father came in from the fields. He went into the barn to put some things away, then came out really fast. He found me in the house helping Mother with dinner, and he said, "Can you come out here for a minute, honey?"

I went outside with him and walked over to the barn. He stopped me before we reached the barn door. He leaned over and said, "Honey, Mittens is dead."

I started crying, and he went in the barn and came out with a little bundle all wrapped up in burlap sacking. He wouldn't let me see Mittens. All he said was that she'd had an accident. I was so upset I didn't ask any more questions.

We buried her at the far edge of Mother's flower garden, then had a sad, quiet dinner.

Later that night I snuck down and sat on the stairs so I could listen to Mother and Father talk. I liked listening to them talk in the evenings.

I heard Father say, "It don't matter how difficult it will be. We're moving."

Then Mother said something in her quiet voice, and Father replied, "No, I don't want you to see it. Mittens killed it and it killed her and tomorrow I'm going to burn it on the trash pile. That will be the end of it. But I want to move. This ain't no place to live."

Early the next morning, before dawn, I got up and went out to the barn. I wanted to see what Father was talking about.

I found it in a corner, under another piece of burlap sacking—a huge rat, three-foot if an inch, black and gray and covered with lice and ticks, yellowed front teeth four inches long, its throat torn out.

My screams woke the whole house.

The following week, Father bought the old Denner place two miles away. Mother really missed her garden, and she reminisced about it for a long time.

TITLE: "My Gift"
AUTHOR: Edward Leech
AGE: 18
OCCUPATION: Laborer, Cunningham Farm Supplies

There's a man in town named Mr. Driscoll. Some people think he's crazy, but we all treat him well. He's old and was born blind, but he's a seer. He's proved it time and again.

He likes to chew plugs of cherry tobacco, so whenever someone wants an answer to something they bring him one and he's happy. With kids, all they have to do is bring him a handful of Bit o' Honeys and he'll do the same.

Ten years ago, when I'd just turned eight, I started worrying about something, so got some Bit o' Honeys from Wentworth's and walked up the hill to his shack outside town.

It was early December and a light snow was falling, but Mr. Driscoll was sitting on his front porch like always, rocking in his chair, his gray beard stained with tobacco juice.

"How you doin', Eddie Leech?" he asked when I was still fifty paces off.

I paused. His blank, white eyes stared at me as he smiled. "And you brought me a present, too," he went on. "I like you, kid."

I sat down on the mildewed, overstuffed chair next to his and handed over the candy. I shivered in my coat, but Mr. Driscoll, he wore nothing but a plaid work shirt and trousers and looked comfy as a clam.

"I got a question, Mr. Driscoll," I said simply.

"Whelp?" he replied.

"My friend Davie said there's no such thing as Santa. Is that true?"

"No," Mr. Driscoll said immediately. "Davie is wrong. Santa is real."

I wasn't convinced. "But how do you *know*?" I asked.

He smiled, unraveled a Bit o' Honey, and popped it in his mouth. He chewed a long time before answering.

"Next year, your grandma will break a hip but she'll get better. In three years the big oak in Uncanny Square will be struck by lightning, but half of it will live. When you're fifteen, you'll find an injured deer by the side of the road and do the right thing. When you're eighteen, Davie will ask Katie Lockwood to the prom and she'll say 'Yes.'" He paused. "If none of those things happen, I'll eat my hat. If three of those four things happen, there is no Santa. If all four happen, there is. In the meantime, take my word for it and believe. I never lie. Any more questions?"

I gulped and shook my head.

Without missing a beat, Mr. Driscoll reached out and patted my head. "Wait 'til you see what Santa got you this year, kiddo," he said. "Now beat it and have a Merry Christmas."

I did, and I believed again.

That year I got a new bike. My dad had been out of work, so I never did figure out how he managed it.

The following year Grandma broke her hip. She got better and lived another six years.

Two years after that, in the midst of a big summer gale, the Liberty Oak in Uncanny Square was hit by lightning. Half of it fell away. They cemented up the wound and the rest of it lived.

Three years later I was riding my bike back from fishing Still Creek all day and came across a leg-shot deer panting in pain by the side of the road. I had my tackle knife, so I cut its throat...I was sick for a week after, but knew I'd done what needed doing.

And now Prom is two weeks off. Davie's a bit homely, but he asked out Katie Lockwood yesterday morning. She wasn't sure...

So I gave her twenty bucks to say "Yes."

I wonder if Mr. Driscoll knew I'd do that, too?

Anyway, it's an early Christmas gift for Davie...even if he wouldn't understand.

And for me, too.

I still believe.

TITLE: "Out of the Blue"
AUTHOR: George Fielding
AGE: 37
OCCUPATION: Farmer

When I was in second grade, Mrs. Young was calling us in from recess when a snake fell out of the sky and smacked her right on the head.

It was a rattlesnake.

She *hated* rattlesnakes.

She had a heart attack and died, right there on the playground.

I never liked Mrs. Young. In first grade we got into an argument about a worksheet on animals. I said a mountain goat was a reptile, and got mad when she said it wasn't. She got mad when I got mad, and things went downhill from there.

Then, a year later, that rattlesnake fell out of the sky and smacked her on the head.

No one ever figured out where it came from. It was just one of those things.

All the kids screamed when they saw her topple, and they screamed louder and ran off in all directions when the snake slithered out from under her fleshy bosoms and onto the kickball field.

But I didn't.

Instead, I went up to her body, gave it a little kick on the shoulder, and said, "Way to get hit by a *mammal*, Mrs. Young."

I love that story.

So do my kids.

TITLE: "Puddles"
AUTHOR: Randy Cunningham
AGE: 14

There's this one thing that happened when I was five years old. It had to do with our next-door neighbor.

I don't remember his name and my parents won't talk about him when I ask. I don't know why. Maybe it has to do with what happened to him.

His name was David Brautigan and he was afraid of puddles. All kinds of puddles. I remember seeing him dodging between them on our street after it rained. If it rained really hard he wouldn't go outside. The older kids used to make fun of him and the adults thought he was crazy. Jenny Sumpkin's probably writing all about that dumb Ben Sparks, the one who hated water, but this guy didn't hate water. He could swim like a champ and loved it. Just puddles. He hated puddles.

This Brautigan guy, he was maybe twelve years old, about the same age as my sister, when we heard him screaming out in the street one day. School had just let out after a monster rainstorm and there were puddles everywhere. He had to take the bus home. He couldn't avoid the walk from the bus to his house, and so he was fit to be tied. But that wasn't why he was screaming.

We all rushed to the front door and Mom barreled past us. She was out in the street like a shot, and so were half a dozen other grownups. And they all crowded around so we couldn't see much, but I remember seeing blood. There was blood everywhere. It was coming front Brautigan's foot. His toes had touched a puddle and were gone, cut off cleanly like the water was acid.

After that he didn't go outside much anymore, even when the sky was blue. And when he did, he never strayed far from the house. I can't say as I blame him. He couldn't run fast without his toes.

TITLE: "The Tapestry"
AUTHOR: Mary Davis
AGE: 41
OCCUPATION: Music Teacher, Uncanny Elementary
School

My Uncle Gideon was an odd duck. He was in The Great War—distinguished himself, in fact—and before that, by all measures, he was as normal as green in spring. But after he got back he was quiet, and no longer liked going out much, and kept to himself. Whatever he'd seen and done overseas had played a number on his mind. He got a job as the janitor for the Uncanny Public Library, and that was perfect for him; he only had to work at night, when he was alone, in a place that cultivated silence even during its busiest hours. So he made a decent living despite his condition.

At home, he liked to garden. Loved it. He had a high-walled back yard filled with flowers. And he was a gentle man who loved his nieces and nephews, so when we visited he made us cookies, and lemonade, and showed us all around the yard. And we loved those visits because he never talked enough to bore us, and let us explore, and play, and chatter to our hearts' content.

My favorite part of the yard was a little alcove of butter-fly bushes. According to Grandma Morris, Uncle Gideon had never shown any interest in butterflies until after the war, but from that point on he kept a soft spot for them. The bushes extended beyond the fenced-in area into a back lot that wasn't his property, but which no one ever bothered, since the house that went with the land had been abandoned long ago. A little path covered in wood chips led to the bushes, and he kept a bench out there among them.

I remember sitting on that bench with him when I was a little girl, drinking lemonade, waiting for the butterflies to land. They came on warm days, when there wasn't much rain...Monarchs, Black Swallowtails, Checkered Whites, Buckeyes, Pearl Crescents...you name it, they all dropped down to visit. And when Uncle Gideon saw them, he'd smile, point them out, whisper their names, and sit very still until they fluttered off again.

"Graceful," he replied, the one time I asked why he liked them so much. "And beautiful. They die if you touch them, they live only a few days, but they are all grace and beauty. Neither lasts long in any one body, but both come back again in others, every year." Then he closed his eyes, took a deep breath, and added, "They're perfect."

I never heard him speak so many words at one time, before or after. And he must have believed what he said, because only out there, on that bench, surrounded by those graceful, beautiful, fragile things, did he ever seem fully content.

Several years later, a man bought the abandoned house behind Uncle Gideon's. His name was Mr. Norberg. He wasn't from Uncanny, which was unusual, but I guess he thought he'd have a go at it here.

Sometimes people do that, but it doesn't always work out.

Well, Mr. Norberg fixed up the house, and boy, did he make a racket, bothering the neighbors by working until all hours of the night. That didn't win him any new friends. And then he started in on the yard, and that proved to be another sticking point, because even though Uncle Gideon saw those butterfly bushes as his, they weren't, really. They were Mr. Norberg's. And Mr. Norberg didn't think twice about tearing them all out and putting in some fancy swimming pool where they'd once been.

Uncle Gideon, he did what he could to reason with Mr. Norberg, but the old cuss would have none of it. Told Uncle Gideon property was property, borders were borders, and it was his right.

Uncle Gideon told him that just because something was a person's right, didn't make *doing* it right. But it was like trying to reason with a wall. An obnoxious wall.

After Uncle Gideon lost his bushes, we spoke with him about planting new ones the following spring. I remember sitting out on his back porch with him when we talked about it—me, and Mother, and my brother Paul, and him. And he said he'd think about it the following year, but that for now summer was almost over, and besides, he didn't have space in his yard...not enough, at any rate. And I remember looking at him as he said that, and seeing a dullness in his eyes that I didn't like, and wondering if he was hurting from the loss more than he let on.

"Even a small bush would be better than nothing," I told him. "I'll get you one myself."

But he patted my arm and said, simply, "I told them they'd always have that place. And now it's gone."

"Who?" I asked. But he didn't reply, and in the months that followed he turned even more quiet than usual, and no longer smiled.

Then one day a neighbor called Mother and said he hadn't seen smoke rising from Uncle Gideon's chimney that morning. Shortly thereafter, Mrs. Schretengoss arrived, quite alarmed, to report that he hadn't shown up for work the previous night.

Sheriff Cobb took a drive over to Uncle Gideon's and found him dead on the back porch, his military uniform on, his bolt-action army-issued rifle at his feet, a bullet through his throat. There was no note. Cobb commented that, oddly enough, a single Monarch butterfly had alighted on Uncle

Gideon's shoulder shortly after his arrival, and remained there until they moved the body several hours later.

*****

It happened for the first time the following year, on the anniversary of his death.

Robbie Snow was biking by the empty house early that morning, delivering papers, when he stopped short. He paused, stared, then proceeded to wake up several neighborhood blocks with his hollering.

It didn't take long for a crowd to assemble in front of Uncle Gideon's property. Word spread fast. Soon, without any exaggeration, virtually all of Uncanny stood gawking at it, me included.

The butterflies had covered every square inch of the house—the walls, the roof, the chimney, the porch. And the front yard, too…all of it: the grass, the driveway, the walkway, the trees. Everything, *everything* was covered with a living, shifting, fluttering tapestry of butterflies—and not just Monarchs and Swallowtails, either. No, there were dozens and dozens of species, including some that could only have come from west of the Rockies, from Mexico, or from South America.

It was thrillingly, unutterably beautiful.

It was also impossible. And not only because of how many, or what kinds.

It was impossible because Uncle Gideon had died on January 7th.

It was the middle of winter.

That was 22 years ago. Every year since then, on the same date, the butterflies have returned. A few years back Mayor Allan proclaimed January 7th a town-wide holiday, so everyone can sit out by Uncle Gideon's house—taking in the sight, drinking hot apple cider and passing around homemade soup—until nightfall, when the butterflies finally, silent as milkweed down, ascend into the shadowed sky and disappear into cold, cloaking darkness.

Oh, and as for Mr. Norberg? After the appearance of the butterflies that first year, he simply up and vanished. No note, no forwarding address, Chevy still in the garage, everything in his house just as he'd left it. There was a search, but it turned up nothing. Eventually his belongings were donated to charity and his house put up for sale. There were no buyers.

No one seemed terribly upset by this. I wasn't either, although I do sometimes enjoy wondering whatever happened to him.

The possibilities are as numerous as the butterflies.

TITLE: "Buddy"
AUTHOR: Freddy Ward
AGE: 7

DADDY GOT A BIGFUT IN THE BAK PASTUR IN A SHED.

HE WONT LET NO ONE PLAY WITH IT. GRAMPA COT IT LONG AGO. HIS NAMES BUDDY. HES REEL BIG AND HE SMELLS FUNY. EVERYWON NOWS ABOUT HIM BUT THEY DONT MIND NONE AND THEY DONT BUG HIM.

HE LIKES APPLES AN PIGS MEET.

AN THATS MY STORI.

TITLE: The Good Job
AUTHOR: Caity Griffin
AGE: 39
OCCUPATION: Waitress

Jessica Walters and I *loved* Halloween. Ever since we were little girls it was our favorite holiday. Neither of us married or had children, but ten years ago, since we missed walking around town and seeing all the decorations and children getting candy, we decided to stroll the cool evening streets anyway, watching the holiday unfold. And every year after that we did the same thing, shivering as the wind blew leaves off the great oaks and maples that lined the sidewalks, smelling the wood and pumpkin smoke, watching the children take hold of the night. For two hours, between seven and nine, Uncanny Valley became *their* town. And ours.

Well, three years ago I walked the dozen doors down to Jessica's house and met her at the door. She was dressed as a witch, and I'd come up with something kind of resembling a mummy outfit (it was made of toilet paper and masking tape). We laughed a bit, talked about our shift down at What's Cookin' at Casey's, compared tips, and headed out.

Jessica was in a fine mood. She'd just been promoted to Head Waitress, and that was good for both of us—she because of the raise, me because she was my best friend and that meant good shifts. And because it was Halloween, of course. We both loved what she called "safe terror," the chance to feel afraid without actually being in danger—like watching a horror movie or reading a good ghost story.

The sun finished setting as we stepped out into the dark, and four blocks away Uncanny Courthouse tolled the hour. Halloween officially began. We started up Pugh Street, headed uphill four blocks, and turned right onto Church Street, which is lined with big, expensive houses and divides Upper Uncanny and the rest of town. Children swept around us like leaves: goblins, devils, scarecrows and fairy princesses. Their laughter was a natural part of the night, and we joined in.

Then, abruptly, Jessica stopped laughing—not gradually, but straight away, like a door had shut between her and me, cutting off all sound.

"Look at that," she said in a low voice. And I looked.

Sitting on the front walkway step of the nearest three-story Victorian, a jack o' lantern glowed brightly. And what a face! I gasped; I couldn't help it. Whoever had carved it had done a very, very good job. It looked like a dead woman, you see. Matted, long hair framed a hollow-cheeked face. Its lips were pulled back, maybe rotted away, exposing too-long teeth. The nose was half-gone, and instead of eyes there was nothing left but empty sockets—painted black, not carved, so no light could shine through. All this in a pumpkin. I'd never seen anything like it. Even Farmer Gill who sells special carved jack o' lanterns every Halloween never had one like that.

I looked at Jessica. She was shaking.

"That's too much," she said slowly, lips trembling. "That's the ugliest thing I've ever *seen.*"

"Yeah, it's pretty bad," I said. "Someone's got a gift, that's for sure." I elbowed her. "Got a reaction out of us, didn't it?"

Reluctantly, Jessica smiled a little. "Sure did. Who lives in that house?"

"It's abandoned," I said. "Remember? The Martsens moved out last year."

"Oh, yeah."

"Come on, let's keep going." I was happy to lead her away. She'd been pretty shaken up, and that surprised me. It wasn't like her to get really, truly creeped out.

We walked on. After a few minutes Jessica said, "I don't know why that hit me so hard. I guess…"

"Yeah?"

She sighed. "It sounds crazy, but that horrible face looked kind of familiar."

"You know any dead bodies?" I asked, laughing. I couldn't help it. But she didn't laugh back.

Slowly, though, she started to relax again. The more we walked, the more costumes and lights we saw, the more she came back to herself. I was glad. Boy, was I. It wouldn't do for a little thing like that to ruin Halloween!

Cold wind howled high up through the tops of trees. In Uncanny Park, across Still Creek, the boy scouts held their "bobbing for apples" contest. Far away, through a copse of willows, we could see the lights and hear the children's laughter, so we went to join in.

We had a great time, watching them play in the deepening night. A full moon shone through passing clouds as they dunked themselves in the rain barrel and tried to bite the floating apples. Parents handed out hot cider and packets of candy corn. Old Mr. Weiss told scary stories.

And as we left, striding over the dark field, passing the swing sets that creaked and groaned, the picnic tables and skeletal jungle gyms, Jessica looked at me and said, "It was a good night. Another Halloween almost over. I wish it was just starting, but that's how things always are…over before you even know they've really begun."

It was when we crossed the small covered bridge that spans Still Creek that she cried out, and I can't say I blame her. For there, sitting on one of the wooden sills overlooking the cold, oily water, was that same awful jack o' lantern, leering at us with its rotted face, expression shifting horribly as the candle inside flickered.

She ran then. She ran and I followed. And I didn't run only to catch her, but also because suddenly, at that moment, the horrible face looked familiar to *me*, too. And I was scared.

I found Jessica sitting on the bench outside Wentworth's Grocery, the place where the old men always play checkers when the weather allows. She had been crying but wasn't any more. Instead she looked at me with sullen eyes and said, simply, "Take me home."

"Why don't you come home with me?" I suggested, placing my hand gently on her shoulder. Halloween was over now. The town was silent and cold and lonely.

"No, thank you. I'm thirty-seven. That's far too old to hide under the covers or cling to other people. There's nothing to be frightened of. It's just some idiot's idea of a practical joke, right?"

"Right," I said, and God forgive me.

"Then take me home and get yourself home safe too, and we'll meet at Casey's for breakfast tomorrow, OK?"

And I took her home, and then I went home, and for us, Halloween ended forever.

I wonder, now, what she must have been thinking on that final walk down the block. Our guts sometimes talk more sense than our brains, and her gut (and mine) was churning. But brains have a way of talking louder sometimes, and that gives them the upper hand.

It was Jake Cleary, the garbage man, who called the police early the following morning, two hours before dawn. Jessica's front door was open, and when he yelled inside she didn't answer.

Sheriff Cobb found her body upstairs—not just in her bedroom, but in two other rooms, too. The only piece of evidence the combined efforts of three precincts turned up was a jack o' lantern, candle burned down to almost nothing, grinning out from the window of her attic cupola. Cobb talked privately to me after I gave my statement, and said, "It had a messed up face that gave me the shivers."

And only later, at the end of that long, long day, as my mind gave way to half-dreams and my gut finally spoke up over that loud, constant voice, did I realize why, possibly, the face on that pumpkin had looked familiar.

What, it asked, *will Jessica look like after two months in the ground?*

TITLE: "My Ghost"
AUTHOR: Richard Martin
AGE: 57
OCCUPATION: Librarian, Uncanny Area High School

I was born on Canon Street. It's a good two blocks up the hillsides of Upper Uncanny—a street lined with old homes known for their high ceilings, gables, lead glass windows, green copper weathervanes and gardens overflowing with cascading ivy and purple flowers.

It was a fine place to grow up. I'm an only child, and I made my own fun when my friends weren't around, but they often were, since my house was a fun place to explore. I never got bored with it. There was always something new to find.

I was fifteen when I discovered the house was haunted.

It took awhile before I was sure that's what was going on. I mean, ghosts are supposed to be like that, aren't they? Elusive. Ambiguous. But that year I started noticing strange things—a shadowy figure that sometimes moved behind the curtains when I was leaving the house, light breath on the back of my neck, high-pitched laughter in the dead of night. Old toys scattered. Oh, and messages on my writing slate: *Remember, I see you, I'm still here.*

I never told my parents. They didn't believe in such things, so why bother? I didn't need a fight, didn't want to be looked at strangely, and besides, whatever it was in that house never seemed to mean any harm.

Years passed. People I thought would never grow old, did. Car models came and went. Concrete replaced the rutted dirt of the side streets.

As for me, I moved across town, rented the top floor of Mrs. Wallace's boardinghouse, became the high school librarian, and settled into a safe and dependable routine.

More years passed. I thought little of ghosts.

And then, one dark November, my father passed away, just four months after my mother lost her battle with cancer. A heart attack, the doctors said. A broken heart, I think.

In all the years since I moved across town I had rarely spent a night in the house of my childhood, but some weeks later, after working ten hours straight making an inventory for the estate sale, I dragged myself up the creaking oak stairs to my old bedroom and threw myself on the dusty sheets of my old bed.

I slept for some time. When I woke it was dark and the moon was at its zenith, the tall houses up and down the street illuminated by a milky glow. Everything was very still. A frost, perfect and untouched, lay on the yards and on the wind-shields of cars.

I breathed softly, and I listened to my breath—waiting. Silence like that always comes when something is about to happen.

Across the room, a white shape slid off the dresser and floated, like a leaf, toward the bed.

Not a second later, laughter, very close and not my own, jerked me up and across the floorboards, out the door, and down the stairs.

At the kitchen table, heart still pounding, I looked at what I held in my hand; at the white, fluttering thing I'd grabbed as I ran.

It was a drawing—a little thing I'd made when I was a boy. I turned it over. On the back, in messy, childish script, I'd written my name, along with, *Mrs. Crenshaw / sixth period.*

I thought a moment, then examined it again—a silly drawing, but one I'd doubtless worked at very hard: a boy sitting on the bank of a stream in green grass, under a

Weeping Willow, a nice bundle of fish on his left side, a brown dog sitting next to him on his right.

Then it came back to me: Mrs. Crenshaw standing before the class, black hair pulled back in a neat bun, all waving arms and boundless enthusiasm. And she, with a flourish, saying, "Draw your perfect day. What you'd like to be doing most in all the world."

Fishing. That was my perfect day, way back when. Fishing with my dog, Sandy, and Dad somewhere nearby downstream, staking out another spot in the early morning sunshine. And Mom waiting at home to help us clean and cook our catch. Damn, but I hadn't thought about that kind of thing in thirty years. I'd drifted away from it, left my dad to do crosswords on the front porch rather than go fishing with me, left my mom to make suppers I often missed. And eventually Sandy got too arthritic to walk with me, and I graduated from school and left. Even though I lived just across town and visited every Sunday, I'd left.

I clenched the drawing in my fist. My hands had a mind of their own. So did my mouth. It said, "I can't remember how to fish. I just can't remember."

I left my perfect day on the kitchen table. I couldn't stand to look at it but I couldn't throw it away. I left the house, too; got in my car and drove back to my dark room at Wallace's. No more nights at home.

No more home.

The next morning, when I returned, the drawing was gone.

Three weeks later, the house empty and sold, I pulled out of the driveway for the last time, just as the early winter night was beginning to fall.

I looked back at the house. Just one quick glance.

A figure was standing in the doorway. A small figure, hand raised.

I knew that figure once. Knew him well.

I don't know him any more.

TITLE: "The Bad Spot"
AUTHOR: Donald Whordley
AGE: 61
OCCUPATION: Farmer

There's a hollow in Uncanny, way down deep behind the dam that flooded out the lower end of town. It's a bad spot. When we was kids the old folks always clammed up when they talked about it and saw us listening. There was precious little we ever found out from them, but it was enough to make us wonder.

Here's what I heard back when I was a tike:

Down past the dark pines at the bottom of the hollow there's a wall of stone. There's a hole in the wall where a gate once was. Past the hole is a bunch of stone steps, and at the bottom of them steps is an old well of black shiny rock.

There's something about the wall and the hole and the steps and the well that ain't right. Especially the well. That's the heart of the whole mess. I know it now.

No one knows when it's from, but the old men from my youth said it was there before the town was settled. Before the Indians, even. Some said it glows sickly colors at night. I wouldn't know that. I only saw it once, and that by day.

They also said it sings, and I do believe that's the case.

Then there's one other thing I overheard when I was eleven. It was dynamite next to everything else I'd learned. I remember it real well, though it was fifty years ago. I don't like to think about it because of what happened after, but there's plenty about life that might best be ignored yet can't be.

And another thing about life: the past always comes around again.

*****

The one time I saw the well was back in my youthful days, before the dam was built, after me and Drake Kelly overheard some men behind the church talking about having some kind of event in that hollow. Reverend Healey was smoking a pipe and talking real low to Eugene Wentworth, Roger Burlington, and my father.

This was late one afternoon after "Spring Cleaning Saturday." Some of the Church Elders spruced the place up once a year, that's all the name meant. But that evening they finished, and Drake come up and got me and said to come on and listen to their talk.

I did. We went together, hiding around the corner on the lee side of the church. And we heard Reverend Healey say, "I got visited twice this week. I don't have long." And my daddy said, real serious, "I guess we could try it. Otherwise…" And Reverend Healey said, "Otherwise I won't be able to keep it out."

Mr. Wentworth, he was a real mean old bastard, but even he showed concern. He said, "Reverend, can't you stay in the church? They can't get you there. The Good Lord will protect you in His House."

But the Reverend said, "I won't hide in the skirts of my religion, Eugene. A man of God must stand in the face of darkness and be His Sword."

"No offense to the Almighty, but we all know it'll kill you anyway, James," said Roger Burlington. "Even if we do try."

"Where's your *faith*, man?" Reverend Healey shot back. "That's no way to talk. Yes…yes, we'll try it. Before it comes out again. Tuesday morning, we go to the well."

*****

A talk like that got our hearts to racing, so what do you think Drake and I did, but follow? We played hooky, scampered out to the hollow, and waited behind a clump of trees near the wall. We trembled a bit, let me tell you. No one else we'd known had ever gone out there before. None of our friends, none of our elders.

Finally the men showed up, my daddy and Eugene Wentworth and Roger Burlington and Reverend Healey himself, carrying a brown leather bag.

I never saw any of them scared before that day, but now they was plenty frightened, even my daddy, all fidgety and huddled and quiet. But with the Reverend in the lead they strode up to the lip of the well and made a circle around it. The Reverend said something in a low voice that sounded like, "If it comes up, hold firm," then opened his bag and took out a silver cross, a vial of holy water, and his big leather Bible.

Then Reverend Healey intoned some things, shook the holy water down the lip of that cold black hole, read some scripture, waved the cross a few times, and spoke something or other in Latin.

"By God, we're seein' an *exorcism*," whispered Drake.

"Nah, that's for Catholics," I whispered back.

"But it *is*, or something like. I wonder if—"

He didn't say nothing else, because then there came a rumbling noise, and the earth shook, and the men clapped their hands together and closed their eyes, and Drake and I grabbed each other and tried not to scream. A horrible stench wafted up from the well, and a strange, high giggle. Wentworth yelped but Mr. Burlington held him firm.

"It's coming!" my daddy hollered. "It's coming up!"

But then things calmed down again and everything got quiet.

The men breathed real heavy for a bit, then Reverend Healey said, finally, "We'll see if that stops it for good," and then, still real pensive, they gathered themselves up and went on home.

Drake and I had to wait a bit before we could follow, so as not to be seen. That was a long moment for us. And it got worse, because just as we got ready to head up the long path to home, Drake cocked his head and said, real strange, "You hear that singing?"

I told him no and dragged him off. I was creeped, and he wasn't helping. We split for our homes when we reached Pugh Street. And I figured that was it.

But next morning Reverend Healey was found dead.

They had a closed casket at the funeral, though that wasn't tradition. I guess the exorcism hadn't done much besides cause that well to belch a bit of evil. And that evil was enough to kill.

*****

Drake disappeared three days later. I only saw him once again before he vanished, and all he could talk about was the song in his head.

"Like angels," he said.

They spent two weeks searching for him, day in and day out. And I couldn't say what I thought. I was too much the coward. I wonder if my daddy suspected I knew something. Sometimes I caught him looking at me funny.

It was three months after they gave up the search, and shortly after Mrs. Kelly came back from the mental hospital upstate, that I saw Drake again.

I was walking home from fishing one evening in early August. The late day was hot and thick and heat lightning flickered on the dark horizon. I was crossing Palmer's back pasture and smelled something rank.

I looked up, and there was Drake.

He was standing a short ways off at the edge of the field by the woods. He was dead. I saw that straight away.

He'd been tow-headed but now his hair hung lanky and black, and his face looked as pale as a dead brookie. And his eyes…even from a distance I could see they'd gone black, with not a smidge of white left.

"Drake," I said, and stood rooted.

He smiled, and there was nothing but black bloody gums. Then he took a step closer.

He didn't mean me a good turn, I could tell. So I got my legs back, I ran and I ran, and I don't remember sleeping for a good three nights, because how do you hide from something like that? And how do you deal with it?

But he didn't come back. Slowly the feel of that meeting faded. Then, four years later, I saw him again. And ten years after that. Always at dusk, always outside. He never aged. He never spoke. And each time someone else disappeared in Uncanny I wondered about that well. And each time I saw Drake I thought of Reverend Healey and what that meant for me.

In the years since I was a kiddo, I can't say I've learned much else beyond what I overheard that one dark day. Maybe when the oldsters up and died they took their learning with them. That's a shame, because it might have saved a few lives if more folks knew what they once did.

Maybe it would have saved mine.

Two nights back there was a knocking at the door. Outside, it was "gloaming time," as Mrs. Gerts calls it. I opened up, and there was nothing but a horrible dead smell and a pool of dark water on the front step.

Last night it came again, and when I opened the door, heart all aflutter, I felt a cold wind and heard a giggle right close by my ear. But there weren't nobody there.

The way I figure it, my time's up. I don't know why I got picked the way Reverend Healey did, or, hell, why Reverend

Healey got picked either, but as my daddy used to say, there's predators and prey in this world, and I guess you don't always have a choice in which you get to be. If you did, hunters'd always come up empty.

Maybe since Drake was my best friend, that formed the connection. Maybe Reverend Healey's best friend up and disappeared when he was young, too. And then, years later, too long for the rest of town to put two and two together, the thing in the well made its move, and only a few scattered old men could even guess how all the pieces fit. Like I'm guessing now.

Maybe it's been like that for a thousand years.

It's a shame. Drake, he was a sweet kid. Before, he never would of done me harm.

I gotta drop this in the mail, then head home. I have a date with my rifle.

Maybe what lives down there is hungry. Maybe just lonely. Either way, it amounts to the same thing.

I don't plan to find out one way or the other.

TITLE: "The Winter Noise"
AUTHOR: Tara Ginger
AGE: 15

Tina and Mandy and I had a sleepover one winter night this past year. Every Friday we stayed over at one of our houses, and we switched houses every time.

This last winter was cold. I mean really cold. There wasn't just snow this past winter, but ice like you've never seen in the Valley. The wind was so feirce it turned the snow to hard little cristals that blew around like darts. If you left your nose uncovered when you walked down the street, it would be all red and raw by the time you got where you were going.

There's a rule that if the temparature falls below seven degrees they can't make us go to school. Well (this was in January) the temparature hadn't been above six degrees for over a week, so we were really happy. I mean, who wouldn't be? How often do you miss a whole week of school because of snow and ice like that? It was a real anomely. So it was a great Friday, since it was after a week of no school and all the weekend still stretched ahead.

That night we stayed at Mandy's house. I don't like staying at Mandy's house because her mom's so strict. I'd never tell Mandy that, but it's true. Tina feels the same way. Mandy's dad doesn't really care what we do. He sleeps like a log. But her mom wakes up if you cough across the house, so after eleven we could hardly talk at all. If her mom woke up she'd come down stairs in her face cream and bathrobe and that would be it. She'd let us have it.

But this time Mandy's parents were away in Boston, and her grandma was in a nursing home now so couldn't baby sit, and we lied to our parents about it, so we had the house to ourselves.

The sleepover was going pretty good. We played some games and listened to some radio, and then we started a fire in the fireplace. Well, the orange light was spooky-looking so we decided to tell ghost stories. And we told each other the hook on the car handle story, and the truck driver flashing his high beams to stop the killer story, and the "Aren't You Glad You Didn't Turn On The Lights?" story, and all those. I'd heard them before, but we were still getting real creeped out.

And that's when we heard the scratching on the window.

We all let out big screems, but then we stopped, I guess cause we weren't really sure what it was. I thought maybe it was a branch, but Mandy said there weren't any trees around her house.

Finally the sound quit. We waited, holding our breath. Then Tina giggled and said, "Your both a bunch of scaredy-cats." And Mandy smacked her arm. And then the scratching came again, except this time it was at the window on the *other* side of the house.

"It's a cat," Mandy said, but I ran into the kitchen and Tina followed. I flipped the light switch but nothing happened. Tina picked up the phone, but it was dead as dirt.

I don't think there was ever a night that lasted longer. We cowered down by the fireplace and every ten minutes or so their came a scratching on a back window, a tapping on the wall, or a knocking on the door. Tina and Mandy and I stopped screeming because we didn't want whatever was out there to know where we were in the house. We held our mouths shut with our hands.

Then, after almost an hour of quiet, just when we started thinking it was all over, there was a SLAMMING on the front door, again and again, followed by a horrible wail that trailed off into a low, gutty moan. And then we screemed again, over and over, and all I remember is that we screemed until we got too tired and worn out to screem any more.

I guess we drowsed then. At least I know I did. And around five in the morning I woke up and when we checked, the phone line was back up and the lights worked again. Tina and Mandy were crying and shaking so much that I was the one who had to call the police.

Sheriff Cobb and his deputies pulled up quick enough. We could see the lights, so pushed back the window blinds. The men were their in the driveway and running up the walk, but they didn't knock on the front door. One of them said, "Oh, Jesus," and then another went round the back and knocked on that door instead.

We let Sheriff Cobb in and I didn't like his face. It was all crumpled and white. And he took off his hat and held it in his hands real tight. And he said, "I want you girls to stay inside, over by this side of the room. I'll stay with you. There's been an accedent."

And Mandy asked, "What does that have to do with what we herd?"

And the officer said, "Just hush now, an ambulanse is on the way."

Soon after that my daddy came to pick me up. He walked around the back of the house and he was pale like the officer, and he said, "Come on now, Tara. We've got to go. But I want you to promise me to close your eyes until I tell you. Understand? You do that, or you'll get a slapping."

Then I said bye to Tina and Mandy and he led me outside. I felt the terrible cold, and when I figured we were at the front of the house I heard men talking, and one said, "Whose going to tell her? When are her folks getting home?"

That's when I couldn't stand it anymore. I opened my right eye a slit, like my brother Bobby taught me.

I wish I hadn't. I should never have done so.

Standing pressed against the front door was an old lady, lips purple, face white, eyes open. She was in a bathrobe and slippers. Her mouth was open too and she didn't have teeth.

And her tongue was blue. And when I saw that, I started to screem, to screem and screem and screem.

Daddy never slapped me for it. But he wouldn't answer any questions, either. Never. But I found out later it was Mandy's grandma, wandered off from the nursing home. That, and their was a track of footprints all around the house, like she'd been circling for a way in, round and round and round until she gave up.

Mandy missed a week of school after that. She don't talk much now.

TITLE: "Don't Tell!"
AUTHOR: Danny Moellers
AGE: 9

I have a secret. I cant tell nobody. That wouldnt do. Miss Gentry told me so. So I keep quiet. But I think a lot. I think about the secret.

It could hurt her if I told. It could hurt me too. So I dont tell. I keep quiet and dont tell no one. But she didnt say nothing about writing down stuff. I cant write good. But its all I can do since I cant tell.

Miss Gentry gives me cookies and lets me sit on her porch. Shes real pretty. I used to think shes twenty or thirty. At first she sat on her porch and called me over every day when I walked to school. At first I didnt answer. Mommy and Daddy told me not to talk to her. They said shes strange. So I didnt. But she smiled so nice and never stopped asking. So one day I went up and said hi. She liked that and gave me lemonade. It was great! It was the best I ever had. She said it was her own resipe.

After that I sat with her every day. Only for ten minutes or so. That way Mommy and Daddy wouldnt worry. And wouldnt no. And she started talking. A little each day. And she said she had seven children. Four girls and three boys. And I asked her where they was. And she got real sad and said they was dead. And I cried and said I was sorry. And she hugged me.

And I learned more about her every day. She said shed come from far away. And did I no England? And that she came from a town in England. And I asked which. And she said it was gone so it didnt matter. And I said that was sad.

But she said it didnt matter so much since she had Uncanny now. And that ever since she found it she was happy. Thats good.

After church one day I went to the sematery. Mommy wanted to see Grandpas grave. And not too far away I found three stones. They all had Miss Gentrys last name. The first names was Mark and Matthew and Richard. And they all lived real long and died in 1869 and 1876 and 1881.

Then I asked Miss Gentry about them. She got real quiet. I asked what was wrong. And she said they was her children. And that the other four died long before them. I laughed. I couldnt help it. I knew she was fibbing me. She was pulling my leg!

But she cried so. I felt real bad. But I said how can that be? Your a young lady! And those people died and got buried long back. She didnt say nothing for a long time. She looked at me real good. I began to feel wierd. Then she got up and walked in the house. She came back with something in her arms.

It was a painting. I asked her to turn it around. She didnt for a minute. Then she did.

It was real old. It was a woman. And it looked just like Miss Gentry. The woman was real pretty.

I asked who was it? She said it was her. Then she turned it over again. She tapped a bit of writing on the back. I looked. It was a date. The date was 1654.

I started to cry. I ran away. I was scared. But I went back. I liked her too much. And she cried when she saw me. She said she was sorry. But she was being truthful. Thats what she said. And she said if I didnt believe her I could look in a mirror with her. Then Id see what she really looked like now. But that it was real bad. Because she was so old.

I asked how old. She said she remembered the Black Death. I asked when that was. She said 1349.

I asked how long shed lived in Uncanny. She said since 1797.

Thats her secret. She said I cant tell no one. But I guess most people no. Some like Mommy and Daddy dont talk to her none. They cross the street to let her be. Others do and come to her for advise.

My secret is different. I like Miss Gentry lots. I tell her so all the time. And I guess shes happy to have me around. Maybe I make her think of her kids. That makes me glad.

One day she gave me a special lemonade. She said it took her four hundred years to get the recipe write and it was different from her normal kind. Before I drank it she told me what it would do. I said that sounded great. So I drank it down real fast. It tasted so good!

So now Miss Gentry wont ever be alone again. When the time is write Ill be with her a long long time. She wont cry anymore!

Thats my secret. I cant tell no one. Miss Gentry would get in trouble. I cant have that. And Id get in trouble too. I know it. Mommy and Daddy fuss about things so. I dont want to get grounded. That wouldnt do.

TITLE: "Best Kept Secret"
AUTHOR: Myra Chase
AGE: 41
OCCUPATION: Homemaker

Oh heavens, so many people have asked over the years why I married Harold Chase. I mean to say, they never asked it like *that*, but I could always tell: "So, *how* did you meet?" "*How* old were you?" "He *did* always like pinochle?" I can read between the lines, and I always do the best I can to shrug it off.

But the true answer is that I married Harry because I was young, pregnant, he was the father, and everyone of authority in my life said it was the only thing to do. In other words, I did the easy thing rather than the right thing. Then, later, raising our child, then children, became the right thing rather than the easy thing, so I stayed when I otherwise would have left.

My goodness, but he *is* a boring man, though. Not a bad man beyond some occasional petty meanness, but a real wet blanket. His idea of a vacation is camping down by Uncanny Dam. Even Cleveland is out of his radius. Gettysburg? Better to read about it than see it. And he's eaten the same ham and cheese sandwich for lunch for the last 21 years. No lettuce. No mustard. Just a potato bun and slabs of meat and cheese from Wentworth's.

I could go on about his clothes, our marital habits, his inane habit of reading billboards out loud, but you get the point.

Well, we all get itchy sometime in life, if life is decent but dull, and I got itchy nine summers ago during the Uncanny Fair. I'd never really felt like that before and haven't really felt like it since, but then again, the circumstances of that particular moment were a bit...unusual.

It was a good July night, not a cloud in the sky, all the stars hidden by the bright lights strung high up in the tent. Harry was off judging the preserves for the food fair, Jessie and Graham were playing on the rides with the Deener twins and their family, and I was eating cotton candy on a bench by the little pond that abuts the grounds.

Then *he* sat down beside me.

I didn't even hear him. I was pulling a stray strand of cotton candy from my hair and cursing quietly, and when I looked up, there he was. I'm a jittery person. Can't stand the horror pictures or Alfred Hitchcock films. But I didn't even jump.

Trying to describe him now is very difficult. Sometimes I work to picture his face and can't do it. Other times it comes in clear. But he was medium height, had a swath of black hair longer than usual for most men, and wore a dark sweater and black pants. When I looked at the sweater out of the corner of my eye it seemed to shimmer.

He was very pale, but not in a sick way, and his eyes, peeking out from behind his hair, flashed.

He smiled, and that's when the itch first hit me.

"You look lonely," he said.

Now, I'm a decent woman, and under normal circumstances I would have assumed the worst and given anyone with such airs a good smack.

Not this time.

"No," I said honestly, "I'm just bored. The family is off having fun and I don't care for jam judging or Zapper rides."

He nodded. Behind his hair, his eyes glittered again. Thinking back, there were no lights and no moon to give them light. We faced a dark, still land; the brightness of the tent was behind us.

"This lake," he said softly, turning to me. "Would you like to hear about it?"

I giggled. I hadn't giggled in years. "What's to know?" I said airily. "Mr. Aires owns it. Fish won't live in it and cows won't drink from it. Probably contaminated by runoff from the Sagamore mines. Nothing in there but skeeters and cattails."

"Hmm. Very good. But I know a bit more. Did you realize no one has ever seen the bottom?"

I shook my head. "That can't be. It's a pasture pond. I'm sure most of it dries up every so often when there's drought."

He shook his head right back. "That's what everyone *thinks*. It's safer that way. A puny polluted pasture pond." He looked around. "It's been a long time since I've been up here."

"Um…where are you from? Plumville?"

He didn't seem to hear me. "The lights, the sky, the grass, the fireflies. Fireflies, especially. Yes, it's good to come back. And a fair is always worth a visit, no matter how small and humble it may be."

I stirred a bit at this, suddenly defensive. I still loved the fair—a holdover from childhood. "I wouldn't call it *humble*," I said sharply. "It's small, yes. Not *humble*. That makes me think of…think of…"

I trailed off, frustrated. He seemed to understand. "I meant no offense," he murmured. "Here, but you do seem bored. Bored *and* lonely. Will you walk with me? I'd like to show you something."

Again, I should have slapped him and made off for the safety of the tent. Instead, he pushed his hair from his eyes and I saw them clearly for the first time. They were green. Beautiful, deep green.

Beyond that I can't describe them. I won't even try.

"Yes," I said. "Let's take a walk."

He smiled broadly and my pulse quickened. He stood up, holding out a delicate hand. The fingers, I noted calmly, were *webbed*. I took the hand without hesitating. My pulse positively raced.

"Where are we going?" I asked.

"Let me lead the way."

And then, as natural as strolling down the driveway to pick up the morning paper, he stepped out onto the lake and I followed. We were walking on water. Holding his hand, it seemed a perfectly normal thing to do, even as I wondered at it.

"This lake," he said, "has been here since before the Great Divide."

I had no idea what he meant. I still don't.

"It's a pond," I argued faintly. "Just a pond."

"Really? Look around."

Aires Pond had become a great body of water. The distant fields stretched out and away toward woods far, far off on the edge of sight.

"I'll be." I'm afraid that's all I could think to say.

"Now look down."

I did, and the darkness fell away. A calm, golden light stirred in the depths, rising up through the water and spreading out as it approached until the whole lake glowed in the still, quiet night.

"Like this," he said, and stuck his face beneath the rippling surface.

Wordlessly (I had decided it was best I didn't talk), I bent down, hands as firm on the water as if it were concrete, and ducked my head under, too.

And then all the world was gold and silver fish, swaying blue and purple plants, great turtles and shimmering minnows, and...and *other* things. Creatures I had never seen before. Some with human faces, some without. All glowing with their own light. And set into the steep, distant stone walls of the lake were doorways, hundreds and hundreds of doorways, inlaid with mother of pearl and cowry, and into them and from them—

I lifted my head, gasping. The man did likewise, and smiled.

"A gift," he said. "A gift for you."

"But why *me?*" I sobbed, the water on my face turning salty.

"Because loneliness comes from discontent and discontent comes from loneliness, and this is something we *both* know."

I wiped my nose.

"For one hour of your life," he said, "would you like to know enchantment?"

I looked back toward the far-distant fairground.

I looked around at the glimmering night lake.

I looked into his fathomless sea-green eyes.

I nodded.

"A gift," I said. "A gift for me *and* you."

"My dear," he said, taking both my hands, "shall we go for a swim?"

*****

Jade was born the next year. Harold hated the name, but I insisted. It seemed *right*, her eyes were so stunningly green.

Harry really doesn't understand Jade, and that irks him, so he no longer tries. Not many other folk do, either, although her older brother and sister love her dearly. They know, as I do, that total love can exist without total understanding.

When Jade was three, she began to swim, and when she swims at night the water around her gives off a faint, golden glow.

"Showing off nonsense," is all Harry says.

When Jade turned five, animals started sitting outside our house, quietly waiting until she went out and touched them all on the head. They do it still.

"We should call the exterminator," Harry insists. "Or my brother, Al." Al is a well-known hunter in these parts. But I won't let him do either.

When Jade was seven, she began to float above her bed when she dreamed, a radiance enveloping her and filling the room. Jessie and Graham love it. All Harry says is, "We should plug her in. Save us lots on the electricity bill."

And then, just a few months ago, Jade and I went for a walk in the fields. She likes walking at night. And it wasn't long before she began dancing, her face full of joy at the quiet, living world all around her. And the fireflies came out from the dark shadows under the trees and circled about her like a streaming garment; a dazzling, shining robe. And as she danced and the fireflies shifted with her motion, the very trees seemed to bend forward, watching.

I wonder what Harry would say about that?

But he won't say anything. He needn't know. Some things, I've found, are best kept secret.

TITLE: "The Sounding of the Sea"
AUTHOR: Frank Fielding
AGE: 58
OCCUPATION: President, Uncanny Valley Historical
Society

When Laura Marshall died of cancer this past spring, I wasn't surprised, but I still felt an empty hole where she'd been in my life. Her sickness had lasted almost two years, and for most of that time we'd all known it was likely terminal. Ben, her husband, spoke little about it, except when he drank (more and more often as she got worse), but Laura was straight about it and saw no reason to hide behind a false front.

But despite her acceptance of the situation, she rarely gave in to despair. I don't know how she kept her spirits up. I visited her every week, and I've seen strong people buckle before, even with a dozen shoulders to lean on, and she didn't. Yet when she did seem down, it was always because of the same thing.

"I'll never see it," she said at such times. "It might as well not even exist."

She and my wife were close friends, just as I'm good friends with Ben. It's nice to have at least one couple you and your wife both get along with, and they were ours. And so I heard her say this often, at lunches and dinners and cookouts and picnics.

Laura meant the ocean. She'd *always* wanted to see it, to feel the waves and sand, to hear the seagulls, to smell the salt on the wind. But there wasn't enough money to go to the seaside—not once in her whole life. Ben worked a small farm and had enough trouble making ends meet even in the best of years.

Then, one evening, after the dinners and cookouts stopped and Laura really fell ill—In a way there was no coming back from, not even briefly—I stopped by Schooner's Bar and found Ben deep in a fourth pint of Schlitz.

I pulled up a stool.

"She's on her way," he said simply. His speech was already slurring, and his eyes looked glassy, dazed.

"What's that, Ben?"

"On her way," he said again. "On her way to the grave."

Well, what can you say to that? Nothing. You listen, that's the thing. It's all you can do.

"And she's off her head," he continued, pale face miserable. "She's losing it. I thought, at the end, she'd at least have her mind. Guess that was too much to ask for."

"Why, Ben? What's she saying?"

"Says she hears the seashore. First it was only at night, but now in the daylight hours, too." He gulped the last of his pint. "Another," he said to Beaker Morgan. "Says she can hear the seagulls, hear the waves, hear the dune grass in the wind. Sometimes all she does is sit there in her chair by the fire, eyes closed, but she's not asleep. She's *listening*. And it's getting harder and harder to pull her out of those spells."

Again, what to say? I bought a beer and took a long pull.

"It's very hard. She's always been so sweet, so good," Ben said, and his voice choked up.

Ben was right. Everyone in Uncanny loved her. Over the years Laura chaired up fundraisers for the library, got a playground built for the children, volunteered at church, tutored kids in writing…none of it for any reason other than to help, to make things better. And I knew from talking with Ben that she sometimes saw to it that families in want got baskets of food and clothing, all anonymously, even though she had little enough to call her own.

And to top it off she was a waitress, so from day to day half the town got one of her smiles, and they stuck with a person from morning to night. She wished no harm on anybody. She gave back all she had. One of the real good ones, that was Laura, and those types are few and far between.

I sighed. "Ben, maybe you could explain…why the sea?"

He cleared his throat and composed himself. "I guess we all have a place we hold dear in our minds, a perfect place. Sometimes folks is lucky enough to visit that place. It could be a summer camp, a hilltop with a good view, a little spot by a lake in the woods, a cottage from childhood. Hers is the seashore, but that's too far…we haven't a car, can't afford the Plumville train. She's never complained—that's not her way—but you've heard her mention it, too, now and again."

"Maybe we could put something together at church," I said. "Hell, a train ticket won't be too much if a bunch of us chip in."

Ben shook his head. "It's too late for that now. Besides, she wouldn't let anyone spend the money on her anyway. I thought I could sell the tractor, but she wouldn't hear of that neither. No, all she's got is her dreams now. That will have to do. But Frank…" He paused, giving me a long, strange look.

"What is it, Ben?"

"Frank, I swear, last night when I came home from the fields…there was *sand* on the floor by the bed. And pebbles. And tiny strands of seaweed mixed in. *All of it still damp.*"

I looked at him, and he looked at me, and hell, this time there was nothing else *either* of us could think to say.

*****

Laura died two weeks later, on November 29. As always when such battles end, those of us who witnessed the long defeat felt a certain relief, mingled with our grief, when it was all over.

The funeral was very well attended. It seemed like the whole town showed up. The overflow extended into the church lobby, through the front doors, and onto the lawn.

Reverend Beckman did a nice job with the eulogy, but half-way through I noticed people seemed distracted. There were murmurs, and a few said things like, "Sounds like waves. Is there a record playing?" I heard it, too.

Well, I was one of the pallbearers, and after the final prayer, as we left the church, I couldn't help but notice how light Laura's casket was. The illness had left little behind.

Then it happened. One moment the six of us were carrying Laura out to the hearse, the next we were on our knees, the brass casket on its side, the *CLANG* of its collision with the sidewalk still ringing in our ears.

"Christ," said Rich Martin, slumped over, face white, "what the *hell* happened?" He was still holding onto one of the handles.

"Language, Mr. Martin!" said Reverend Beckman, horrified. "Consider *where you are.*"

"No, he's right," said Max Creevy, getting to his feet behind me. "It got all heavy! What *was* that?"

Ben Marshall was in a grief-induced panic. "Get her up! This *can't* happen! Come on, damn it! Please!"

We got our bearings, steadied ourselves, then lifted the casket, staggering under a new weight. "Do you hear that?" Rich asked. "Something sliding and shifting. Like shale or...or glass or something. From inside."

We listened. We heard.

We set the casket down again.

It hadn't taken long for the crowd to reappear. Families heading out to their cars returned.

"Take it back inside," said Reverend Beckman. "Quickly."

"Laura," Ben said softly, over and over. "*Laura.*"

We couldn't stop him. In a frenzy of sorrow and shock, he pushed us away and dropped to his knees. He snapped back the clasps.

He opened the casket.

Some people experience rare moments when everything they believe is challenged. Or at least shaken up. Those moments stay with them. Surprise, *real* surprise, is an exotic thing not soon forgotten.

All of us at Laura Marshall's funeral now know that to be true.

Laura's body was gone. In its place, a thousand spiral seashells lay in a white, glistening pile.

Slowly, gingerly, we moved in for a closer look.

For a long moment that defied time, no one dared breathe.

Then, tentatively, first one person, then another, leaned forward to pick one up.

*****

Laura Marshall's body was never found. Yet if you go to any home in Uncanny, any home at all, you can rest assured the people who live there have one of Laura's shells—either placed on a mantle on proud display or carefully tucked away in a cedar chest or scented drawer.

And every now and then, if they're like me, they take them out, admire the coral-white sheen and mother-of-pearl enamel, then hold them to their ears.

And what they hear isn't the dull throb of blood amplified by hollowness. No. It's seagulls crying, dune grass rustling, waves crashing on sand...

The sounding of the sea.

TITLE: "Miss Jennings' Family"
AUTHOR: Karen Fitzroy
OCCUPATION: Housewife
AGE: 47

Miss Jennings used to teach piano in her parlor. For years, all the little girls in Uncanny went to her for lessons. It was something of a tradition. Hating them was also a tradition, and I don't know that anyone who ever took her lessons kept playing playing later in life.

We hated the lessons because we hated Miss Jennings. That sounds mean, but it's true. And if you asked any one of us why, we'd probably each have a different reason. Something was just a little *off* about her. For me, it was her smile. It was too wide, too quick, showed too many teeth… and everything above that smile was dead. Her eyes, in particular. There was something wrong with them. Sometimes, in the midst of her cheeriest compliment, her eyes would look like the eyes of a shark.

But still our mothers made us go, and paid Miss Jennings twenty dollars a month.

She was a lady on the far side of middle age, a spinster, and her parlor reflected that. Too much lace, too many pink satin pillows and delicate porcelain tea cups. And those *dolls*.

Everyone commented on her collection of dolls.

There were a good lot in the parlor—maybe three-dozen—but in the little bedroom off the upstairs hallway were *hundreds*. All makes and models. All shapes and sizes. Porcelain dolls and rag dolls, wooden dolls and plastic dolls. Dolls from all over the country and all over the world.

I suspect Mother wanted me to learn piano but didn't particularly like Miss Jennings either. And of course there was gossip—something about a man, a broken heart, and all that. From what I heard as a little girl, Miss Jennings started collecting dolls right after that ended, and her piano lessons allowed her to add to her collection. Our mothers warned us not to touch them, and even though we were little girls who *loved* dolls, none of us ever wanted to anyway.

When I was ten, my friend Sarah Rice and I had lessons together with her every Monday after school. Things went fine, or as fine as could be expected, until after Thanksgiving had come and gone. The week following, we were still a bit peppy from the days we'd had off. Usually we didn't talk much to Miss Jennings unless we had to, but Sarah, who was in fine mettle (and who could be mean enough when she wanted), got bold and said, "Miss Jennings, did you have a good Thanksgiving with your family?" knowing full well she had none.

I held my breath, waiting for that toothy smile to falter.

It widened instead. "Oh *yes*, dear!" Miss Jennings said, clapping her plump hands together. "It was *wonderful*. I cooked *two* turkeys, enough for everyone! The whole family celebrated. We had such a fine time. How was yours?"

That threw Sarah off. "F-Fine, thank you, Miss Jennings," she said softly.

At the end of the lesson Sarah had to trek upstairs to use Miss Jennings' pink, talcum-scented bathroom: too much lemonade at her grandmother's. While I packed up my music in my little folder, I could feel Miss Jennings staring at me. I didn't want to look at her, so kept my eyes down.

A dog started to bark next door. Miss Jennings' neighbor, Mr. Bryant, had recently bought a German Shepard. Its bark was loud and long and went on and on.

Out of the corner of my eye, I saw Miss Jennings' head snap up.

"Two weeks now," she said cheerily. "Two *weeks* Mr. Bryant has had that dog, and he *never* minds it. Poor thing!

But I *am* afraid it will interrupt our practice time. We can't play if we can't concentrate, now can we?"

I finally looked at her. Miss Jennings' smile was wide, gleaming white teeth stained with the pink lipstick she used to paint her gash of a mouth.

After ages, Sarah returned. She was shaking.

"Thank you, Miss Jennings," she said, and pulled me out the front door without another word.

*****

"What *happened?*" I asked as we hurried home in the falling evening light. Sarah was flour-white.

She shook her head.

"Come on, now," I said, stopping. "Spill it."

"Fine. Fine! Just keep walking."

We walked on.

Sarah swallowed. "I went upstairs to the bathroom, and the door to the room with all the dolls was wide open. I mean, you know how it's usually only open a crack?"

I nodded. Once in a great while I had to use her bathroom, too.

"Well, I couldn't help it. I was curious, so I looked in. And there was...there was something wrong."

She kicked a rock down the sidewalk. I waited.

"Karen, there was *food* on their mouths! On *all* of them. Mashed potatoes, grease, bits of turkey, cranberry sauce...and on a little stand by the door was a plate full of turkey bones."

My hands went cold.

"I'm never going back there," Sarah said. "Never."

But we both did. Our mothers wouldn't listen.

*****

Just two days later I saw Mr. Bryant waddling down the street with a hammer in one hand and a bunch of flyers in the other. I stopped as he nailed one to a telephone pole.

"What's that, Mr. Bryant?" I asked.

He grunted, breathing hard. He never walked anywhere unless he absolutely had to. "Dog's missing," he said. "You seen a pure-bred German Shepherd skulking around?"

I shook my head.

The following Monday Sarah and I did our best to show Miss Jennings what we had learned during the previous week's practice. Sarah, sullen and quiet, looked like a rabbit about to run. I just did my best to get through the hour without thinking too much about anything.

Miss Jennings was as cheery as ever. "*Beautiful,* girls," she said. "*Wonderful.* No, D *flat.* Yes. That's right. Try it again."

A gentle snow had started to fall. I could see it moving silently down the sky through the window. I wanted to be out there, running in it, catching my white breath in my hand and the flakes on my tongue. Instead…

Miss Jennings gave my hand a sharp slap, her smile never faltering. "*Again,* Karen!"

The house, save for our hesitant playing, was *very* quiet. So was the world outside.

At the end of the lesson I found, to my horror, that I, too, now had to use the bathroom. Too much hot cider with my after-school snack. I'd never make it home in time.

When I asked, Sarah shook her head violently, but I ignored her.

I walked up the creaking steps, leaving Sarah with Miss Jennings, and passed slowly by the bedroom door that Sarah had found wide open the week before. This time it was shut.

I used the bathroom, walked quickly back down the hall, then paused.

On the doorknob to the closed bedroom door, a small, dark stain blemished the shining brass.

I touched it. The stain was dry. It looked like maroon paint.

My mind stopped thinking. I didn't *want* it to think. Still not thinking, I turned the knob and pushed the door open.

Three hundred dolls stared back at me with glassy, dead eyes. All of them were smiling. I took a step forward. Their smiles were…a bit too wide. A bit too *dark*.

One more step, and I saw why.

I ran screaming down the stairs, stumbled into the parlor, and dragged Sarah away. Miss Jennings lunged forward, eyes wide, teeth gleaming—she must have guessed what I had seen. Laughing, she reached forward and tore out a hunk of my hair. I yanked the front door open, and then we were out in the cold, snowy darkness, screaming and screaming, as she screamed and screamed behind us.

*****

They took Miss Jennings away and we never saw her again. There was a trial, and we testified, although they kept us in the dark about all the things the police discovered. On the stand, Sarah told about the dolls and their turkey dinner. I told about their bloody mouths, blood-stained dresses, bloody hands, and the dog collar lying on the stand by the door.

A year or so later I heard Mother talking about Miss Jennings with some of her bridge group. She used the word "unspeakable" four times in one minute.

Sarah and I gave up playing piano. No one ever questioned why. We took up needlework instead.

TITLE: "Nihil Obstat"
AUTHOR: Karl Goodwin
AGE: 73
OCCUPATION: Mine Foreman (retired)

I was nine when I found the underground spring at the back of our property. It was at the end of an old dried-out stream bed and built up into the hillside by the edge of the woods with square-cut rocks. Even so, it was mostways hidden by brush and bramble. I heard the trickle. It was August and the air was thick and still. That's how I found it.

The trickle was small and I couldn't see there was much to it. The water ran into a little underground bowl about a foot deep and two feet wide, then disappeared. Curious, I walked around the other side of the hill and found more stone bricks behind the dirt and moss. I gave them a shove and they fell in. And there was the stairway.

I guess it was an old underground springhouse. Probably dated back to when Town got founded in the 18th century. Well, what's a kid to do? They love hidden things and running water and old places and staircases. So I went back to the house, stole Daddy's oil lamp, and crept down those cut stone steps into wet darkness.

They wound down into a small stone room fifteen or twenty feet below ground. The spring water in the basin I'd seen above ran into a smooth gully in the wall and across a rough-hewn channel in the floor before collecting in a deep pool at the far end. The room was cool and dark. I shone Daddy's lamp around, trying to see more. There wasn't much, except the coffin.

That gave me a start. I fell back a bit, my heart jumped a tick, then I settled down. I guess I wasn't too afraid. Mother's funeral had done a number on how I looked at death.

Some kids get a real scare from that sort of thing—what my sis called a "dark turn"—but not me. It had hardened my heart instead.

The coffin was old. A sure relic. It lay on the floor against a wall on the far side of the channel, all covered with white webs of nitre and black streaks of rot. I moved closer and saw it was wooden and full of worm borings and a little caved in.

I ran my jacket sleeve across the wood and coughed as dust filled the close air. On the lid, in big, carved letters, was a date and some writing:

1764

IN HOC SIGNOS VINCES

Well, *that* was something, even though I couldn't read Latin. So after a quick moment of thought I leaned down and jerked off the lid.

It fell apart in my hands. A wretched stench rose up behind it. Gritty, stinging dust struck my eyes. I stumbled back, sneezing and gagging, and when I finally looked in, the first thing my bleary vision focused on were the teeth.

The *teeth*. In a face blackened and twisted with age and decay they gleamed like a beacon, as brilliant and white as untouched snow.

The thing in the coffin was little more than a skeleton, clothed in the tattered remains of an old colonial coat and breeches. He looked like a Revolutionary War soldier, like in one of the historical paintings. Dried, shrunken skin covered the bones of his hands, and those were neatly folded across his chest. Hollow eye sockets stared and a distinguished nose crumbled above the teeth—the *fangs*—sharp as straight-razors and long as my fingers.

I guess if I'd been older I'd have questioned it, but I wasn't, so I believed it was a vampire without thinking twice.

Thing is, the vampire was deader-looking than I'd thought possible. Not like in the stories.

Then I noticed the stake.

His hands weren't just folded on his chest—they were grasping a stump of wood stuck deep in the center of his ribcage.

Now this did give me pause. I'd read enough to know that if I meddled around and brought him back, I myself would be a good target. And they'd never find my body, either. If, even, pulling out the stake would do any good. I wasn't sure.

But again—I was nine years old. Louder than my worry was a voice that said, *Imagine what you could ASK him. Imagine talking to a REAL VAMPIRE. Imagine. Imagine...*

I jerked the stake out with a big, two-handed tug. It yanked the body up a bit with it, then slid out with a sifting of dust.

The result was instant. The skin grew back and the whole body writhed like snakes until what was left was pale, starved, empty, but *alive*: a man with long, blond hair, ta-loned, delicate fingers, and eyes black as pitch, with a pinprick of glowing red deep in the center of each. And then the mouth began to move.

A voice like wind through winter reeds murmured, *"Help...me...rise."*

I leaned down, got a hand under its shoulder, and pulled it upright. The fangs clacked together feebly. A black tongue prodded each point. The body shivered.

"Mussssst...drink..."

"Will that bring you back?" I asked softly.

"Yesssss."

"And then you'll kill me."

A low growl issued up from the corrupted throat. *"No need...ratssss...catssss...deer...beastssss. I will...REWARD you."* The red fires flared in its eyes, then tamped down again.

"I won't kill for you," I said softly. "I can't. I don't even hunt. And then you'll move on to people, even if you spare me, and I have too much kin around to risk it."

Silence, but for a faint hissing. Then, slowly, a white hand capped with yellow talons rose up and grasped my shoulder. Even today I have the scars from those fingertips, although I felt no pain.

"When age strikes you, return to me. When all that you love is carried away, return to me. Then...Time will die, and we will live."

Not knowing what else to say, I could only nod.

"Replace...my...bane. I...ACHE."

I looked at him, then at the stake I still held in white-knuckled fingers. I didn't know what a bane was, not for sure, but I could guess.

With a grunt I shoved it, hard and true, back into his fish-belly chest.

I didn't watch what happened, though I heard it. The racket was awful. By then I was running away, out of that chamber and up the steps into the bright sunlight of a late-summer afternoon.

Later, I bricked up the wall again. I put brush and moss over it. I worked until the sun began to set, all the time panting, *Never...Never...Never...Never.* And I never *did* go back. Not once. Not ever.

That was sixty-four years ago. Now my kin are all dead and moved away. Friends, too. Last month, cancer carried off my wife like Mother so many years before. My children don't know me anymore. Margaret, the closest, is seven hundred miles distant as the crows fly and has a husband who won't let her visit. My mind wanders; I forget the names of things. Then yesterday I coughed up blood.

Blood.

Somewhere along the line I taught myself a bit of Latin. Now I know what the inscription on the coffin lid says.

I don't presume to understand much of life, except that it ends…a bitter truth at best.

Yet that underground room is still there, quiet and cool. I don't doubt it for a moment.

Omne ignotum pro magnifico est.

I must decide. The time, at last, is now.

When I write another line, the decision will be made…

Ad vitam aeternam.

TITLE: "I Got a Secret"
AUTHOR: Brian Fields
AGE: 28
OCCUPATION: Head Janitor, Uncanny Area High School

"I got a secret."

Kenny Milwood smiled as he said it. A fleck of drool ran down his chin. Seven years have passed and I still remember his damn drool. He was like a slobbering, oafish Saint Bernard.

"Sure you do, Kenny." I didn't stop mopping. We still had six classrooms to do, including the science lab, and that always took more time and effort.

"I got a secret."

Old Kenny was slow, otherwise I would've let him have it good. He'd been saying that for over an hour, since the start of shift.

"I got a secret."

"Shut up, Kenny, OK? I'm tired and I want a smoke."

"I got a secret."

I stopped mopping. "Fine! What's your secret? I'm dying to know. C'mon, fill me in. What is it?"

The old man just shook his head. "Not telling!"

"No wonder you're a janitor."

"Hey, that's not nice."

"I'm sorry," I said. And I was. It was a low blow—no shame in hard work, my old man used to say. And by the books, Kenny was head janitor at the elementary school—my boss, in other words—so what did that say about me? Even if I was fifty years younger?

"You really not going to tell me?" I asked, going back to my mopping while he washed the blackboard. "You wouldn't say you got a secret if you didn't want to tell someone."

Kenny shook his head. "Nope! Not now. Maybe later."

I grunted. "Sure. Maybe later."

Kenny squeezed the chalky sponge into the bucket. "I got a secret."

*****

The next afternoon Kenny found me just as I was starting my shift. It was late afternoon, the kids long gone for the day.

"I got a secret," he panted, pawing at my shirt.

"Kenny, if you don't—" I started, then got a good look at him.

He was breathing real heavy, like he was having trouble catching air. And he looked pale, too. And sort of sweaty.

"You OK, Kenny?" I asked.

He shook his head. "It's the secret," he said real fast. "The secret!"

I helped him to the janitor office in the basement. I got him a cold glass of water and some crackers. He drank the water but left the crackers. His eyes were real wide. You could see the whites all the way round, and that's not good.

"All right, Kenny, now tell me what's going on."

He shook his head. "Can't."

"Sure you can. You're a grown man. Nothing's gonna hurt you."

But he shook his head again. "It'll *kill* me," he muttered, wiping his nose and staring at the floor.

I couldn't believe it. Someone—one of the kids, maybe—must have threatened him. Or maybe one of the teachers. Or someone down at Schooner's, where he liked to unwind every Friday. He was what they call gullible, likely to believe whatever anyone told him. And he couldn't tell the difference between funning and real, neither.

But usually most people in town was nice to him. Even mean folk usually draw the line at having sport with a halfwit.

"Who did this, Kenny?" I asked softly. "You let me know who scared you and I'll take care of it. Promise."

This upset him even more. "*Nonononono!*" he cried. "Then you'll get it, too! You'll get it an' I'll get it! We'll both be done in! Done in real good!"

He was breathing hard again. A thin line of drool ran down his chin and landed on his shirt.

I thought a moment, then said, "Tell you what, Kenny. You tell me a bit of it, but not the person's name. That'll make you feel better. And we'll take it from there, huh? Talking always makes a person feel better."

He considered this, and his breathing slowed again. "But...But I gave my *word*," he said. "I *promised* I wouldn't tell."

"But that's where it's OK, see?" I said soothingly. "You can tell me the *gist* of the secret, but without any names. That way no one gets hurt. How's that sound?"

I could tell he liked the idea. He pursed his lips and scratched his head in a way that said he was giving in.

"OK, Brian," he said at last.

"Let's have it, then."

His face screwed up. Then he said, "There's someone killing dogs and cats, Brian. *Lots* of 'em. *Burning* 'em. An' I don't like it! An' just the other night I saw him burning a cow, too! An' it was still alive. Oh, Brian, it was *real* mean, killing something like that so." He gave up holding back his tears. He wept loud, like a little boy who's skinned his knee.

I didn't exactly put my arm around him, but I gave his shoulder a squeeze and did what I could. And all the time I was thinking about what I'd heard around town the last few months: missing pets, strange fires, burned bodies of animals found back in the woods...

"You *saw* this person killing that cow, Kenny?" I asked gently.

He nodded, snuffling.

"Kenny," I said firmly, "you gotta come clean with this. You don't want more nice animals to die, do you? Sheriff Cobb will take care of it, if you've got a name you can give."

"No! No, you promised! No, I won't tell! I won't tell! *It's a secret!*" He leapt to his feet, but I held him back so he couldn't run. He was strong, and it took some doing.

"Fine, Kenny, fine!" I forced him to sit again. "Just tell me one thing. Can you do that?"

"Maybe," he said slowly, panting.

"Is it someone you know?"

Just as slowly, he nodded. "I gotta go now, Brian. We got work to do. I shouldn'ta said nothing. I don't want no trouble!"

He grabbed his tool belt and bucket, and this time I let him go.

*****

That night I thought long and hard. I figured I'd tell Sheriff Cobb and he could have a crack at Kenny. I didn't like doing it, but those killings had gone on for quite a spell, and if more happened, they'd be on me now, too. I decided to take a walk down to the police station the following day.

The next morning Cobb took half a page of notes, smoked two cigarettes, and said, "I guess we'd better go have a talk with Kenny Milwood. We'll be as easy with him as we can."

I nodded. Together we drove over to the school. It was Saturday, so the building would be empty except for him.

133

I unlocked the door. We checked around. No Kenny. We checked the lounge, the front office, the classrooms, the janitor office… nothing.

"Maybe he didn't show today," I said. "He was pretty shook up."

Sheriff Cobb wrinkled his nose. "What's that smell?" he demanded. "Smells *awful.* Smells like—"

We were passing the auditorium and I got a big whiff, too. It *was* awful. I pushed open the double doors.

The stench was overpowering. We walked on down the right-hand aisle, and it only got worse.

Then I saw him.

Kenny was on the stage, or what was left of him, sitting on a prop chair, head thrown back. I could tell it was him because of his gold teeth, but beyond that—

He'd been roasted—burned down to black, charred skin and white bone.

Sheriff Cobb, handkerchief to his face, took one close look and threw up. I remember thinking, *I bet this is the first time that ever happened to him,* then I leaned over and yarked on my boots.

They never found the person who did it. That haunts me as bad as the memory of Kenny up there on that stage. But what haunts me worse, what keeps me up until all hours pacing, scared, like a trapped animal, is what *else* we saw…

A set of little footprints, black with ash, leading away from the husk of Kenny's body.

An elementary school. Jesus Christ.

That was nine years ago. I work at the high school now. Head Janitor. I've moved up. But I don't like kids no more.

I keep thinking to myself, every time one of them smiles at me, *He's the right age. She's the right age. It could be any one of them. They'd be old enough now.*

God, those smiles. Those awful, awful smiles…

TITLE: Lillian Sweeney's Music
AUTHOR: Grace Murray
AGE: 44
OCCUPATION: Seamstress

When I was a little girl, my hero was my grandfather. He was a good man. Everyone in Uncanny respected him. My mother and I lived right down the street from him, so for nine years I clung to his coattails. He showed me all kinds of things because he knew all kinds of things: how to catch a chipmunk with your bare hands, how to charm rattlesnakes, how to pet wild deer without scaring them away, how to spell, how to ride a bike, how to tie two dozen kinds of sailor's knots, how to find arrowheads in the fields, how to douse for water. And he was kind, too. He sang to me when I was sick, made me homemade cards for my birthday, found little treasures and presents for me that he knew I'd love: Civil War bullets, robin egg shells, coins from the 18th century, Luna Moth wings, empty bees' nests, clamps for pressing flowers…

Then, one day shortly before my tenth birthday, Grandpa came in for his Sunday morning coffee and chat and looked especially serious. I hardly ever saw him look that way.

My mother knew right away something was wrong.

"What is it, Pop?" she asked, setting his favorite chipped coffee mug down on the kitchen table in front of him.

He smiled, but it was strained. "Well, kid, I'm hearing the music," he said.

Mother's breath kind of hitched in her throat. She sat down hard. I think if the chair hadn't been there she would have dropped to the floor.

"Are you *sure*, Pop? I mean…are you *really* sure? You're not sick at all. You look hale as ever."

"That don't make a difference, Dear," Grandpa said simply, and took a good, long swig of his coffee. "There's no mistaking it and there's no arguing it."

Mother got a strange look on her face. Suddenly she turned to me and said, very sharply, "Grace, you leave the room now."

I started to argue, but she'd have none of it. Then Grandpa nodded at me and said, "Honey, we'll talk about it later. Mind your mother and don't worry none."

So I left. I went outside and sat on the porch steps.

*****

An hour later, maybe a little less, Grandpa came out and sat down on the step beside me. I was angry and scared. I didn't want to talk.

"Now, now," he said gently. "It's not that I didn't want to talk to you. It's just that your mother had quite a turn, and I needed to iron things out with her. She's a bit better now. So now *we* can have a talk, if you'd like."

I hesitated, then nodded.

"Let's go for a walk."

We stepped out onto the cracked cement sidewalk and my little hand slipped into his big one, a familiar fit.

"I want to tell you a story," said Grandpa.

I looked up at him, frowning.

"What kind of face is that?" he said. "This is a good story. It'll help you make sense of what's upsetting your mother. OK?"

I nodded.

"All right." He cleared his throat. "Way back when, years ago, a beautiful young woman lived up on Arcadia Street in a tall house left to her by her parents. Her mother and father had passed on, her husband was killed in a mining accident, so all she had left was a sweet little boy that was her pride and joy. Her name was Lillian Sweeney. His name was Colin.

"Lillian didn't make much money, but brought in a bit extra with her music. She played the violin, sometimes in a quartet with three friends, sometimes alone. She played at parties and weddings and funerals and other special events. That gave her enough to live comfortable enough with her little boy.

"Then, during a very bad winter, influenza ravaged the whole country. People of all ages were struck down. Hundreds of thousands ended up in the hospital. Many died, especially the elderly and the young. The flu hit Uncanny Valley hard, and Lillian's little boy was one of the first to go."

I squeezed Grandpa's hand hard. He squeezed back.

"Well," he continued, "Lillian was distraught. No one could bring her out of her grief. Colin was buried on top of Cemetery Hill, and she took to playing her violin for hours and hours by the side of his little tombstone.

"The music was indescribably beautiful but also terribly sad. Everyone in town could hear it, borne down on the wind to the streets below, and it most broke their hearts. We all lose someone we love in life if we live any length of time at all, and that music reminded them of their loved ones, now dead and gone. But no one asked her to stop. She needed the music and everyone else realized, in some strange way, that they did, too.

"But one night in February, a windy, storm-laden night, the coldest night of the year, the music stopped. My father and some other men thought they should go up and check on Lillian. They would have done so before, asked her to quit and come in from the cold, but they knew nothing they said would have done any good.

"So they went up the hill in the howling dark, all bundled up, and there she was, frozen, slumped over her child's grave."

"Oh, no!" I cried. "Oh, Grandpa, why are you telling me this? That's terrible!"

"I'm sorry," said Grandpa, "but you need to know. Should I go on?"

I nodded.

"Lillian is gone, but her music continues. Only thing is, the people who hear it, they die soon after. Not *everyone* hears it when their time comes, but those sensitive to such things have sworn it's true. My daddy did, and so did your Uncle Scott. They heard it for days, haunting and sad and beautiful, too. And then, soon after, they slipped away."

"So it's like ghost music?"

"Something like that. How I see it, it's a gift. A way of easing us out of our lives. Lillian was a kind woman, and we all liked her. Yes, it's a gift. I'm sure of it."

I thought a long moment. We walked in silence. Then I stopped cold. "Grandpa," I said, "did you hear the music? Is that why Mother's upset?"

He led me over to a bench and sat me down. "Yes, kiddo. I've heard the music. Heard it for two days now."

I burst into tears.

"Come on, now," he said. "That's just the way of things. It's been a good life. And remember, it's a gift. It gives me a chance to say goodbye to everyone proper."

"But maybe it's just *normal* music you hear! Like a band playing somewhere. Or a record from someone's house!"

"Can you hear it now?"

I listened. I listened as hard as I could. Then I shook my head.

"I can," he said simply. "It's clear as a bell."

And he spoke on, comforting me, and when he died in his sleep two days later, it really *did* help, getting to say goodbye.

*****

I've written all this, after so many years of keeping the truth of it close to my heart, because yesterday I woke up, walked outside into the glorious late spring morning, and heard the music, too.

There can be no mistaking it: a violin, perfectly in tune, its music clear as a bell on every breeze and current of air, its source impossible to pinpoint. And terribly, indescribably beautiful.

But that's not all. I called my best friend, Cheryl Butterworth, and *she* hears it. So does Harry Ward, down at Wentworth's. So do Norton Weiss and Marlene Turner's son, Jeff, and Karen Fitzroy and just about everyone else I talk to.

For the first time since before her death, all of Uncanny can hear Lillian Sweeney's music.

What on Earth is going to happen?

TITLE: "A Warm Glow"
AUTHOR: ?
AGE: 18

I read once of an old belief that if a woman sees a ghost while pregnant, she'll beget a seer. The book said that in some parts of the world, laden women go walking in grave-yards at night, beating graves with sticks. They know the value of having such children in their lives.

This town begets strange things, too. Who can say what Uncanny Valley must have seen? But I bet it *wanted* to see what it did, to make sure it got a special brood. And I was born here, so it begat me. I belong to it. I'm part of it.

And, oh, I was born cold. Cold, cold, cold. I been cold all my life. There's nothing anyone could ever do to warm me up. It's like a hole inside me that can't never be filled. I got ice water for blood and frost for breath. That's my anger, too: cold. So that's why I like fire.

On the flip side, Daddy's anger was always boiling hot. When riled he was handy with his fists and with the hickory, raving and heartless, face a red, burning mask of fury.

And now he's ashes.

I first took note of my skill when I was five. I learned I could snap my fingers and torch mosquitoes and flies so they fell burning from the air like little meteors. At night it was beautiful.

I thought my new trick was something special. All that missing heat, it funneled into my fingertips. Finally, I'd found it!

I ran and showed all my little friends, but they wouldn't have none of it. They turned away and was scared and made fun. And soon they forgot all about me and didn't come by no more.

Daddy never found out what I could do. He just figured I was odd, a sullen reject who kept to himself. So at night, when I was a little older, I started going out in the deep woods and he never thought a thing of it. I practiced. I got better so I could burn more than mosquitoes and flies. Mice and squirrels, then rabbits and raccoons, then bobcats and fox and deer. Oh, and birds on the fly. Those are the best.

I only ever killed one person, back when I was nine. That person, he saw me flame Miss Maxwell's dog. What else could I do? It's bad enough no one here talks to me. I sure as sugar wasn't going to let them lock me up.

For my sixteenth birthday, I took out a bear. You should have seen it trundling through the woods and fields like a great torch, breaking trees, until it collapsed in a heap and blazed like a bonfire of flesh and bone.

And every time I made a fire I felt a little warmer, like I'd put on a sweater after standing naked in the middle of winter. That cold, that horrible cold, it was pushed back...but only for a few hours.

It was never enough. I started in on dogs and cats after the woods started thinning out. That's not easy without getting caught, and I fear I'm getting sloppy...though of course that doesn't matter much now, anyway.

Yesterday I turned eighteen. I graduate high school in two weeks, but there's little for me here. I want to leave, yet Uncanny often has a way of keeping its own where they are. I sure as heck don't want to stay. It made me, but it made me bigger than it, too.

So I'm taking the bull by the horns, as my late father used to say.

Oh, yeah. My father. I burned him because he hit me one too many times. It isn't smart for a father to do such a thing when a son grows up. Daddy had no idea what hit him back and nobody's missed him down at the mill. And again, even if they did...

Anyway, at such a time in life a man begins to wonder about his place in the world. For me, the outside world calls. I know it's coming—or that I'm coming for it.

But first things first.

I been practicing on forests way back in the wild. I'm ready. Holes must be filled. Ice must melt. What begins must end.

Then I'll move on.

Uncanny Valley…it's going to burn with *such* a warm, warm glow.

TITLE: "The Ritual"
AUTHOR: Benjamin Driscoll
AGE: ?
OCCUPATION: ?

There's a shadow being cast. I know it like everything I've ever known. A storm's coming. All towns have to face it, come sometime or other. It comes, and things change. That's the ritual.

I've been blind since the day I was born. But I can feel it in the air and smell it in the earth.

Static ripples through my dreams. Electricity sizzles between my ears.

I'm a seer. They all know it. They've come to me since I was six, when I predicted the War. I'm not usually wrong.

I could tell them. They would listen. But a ritual is a sacred thing.

This one is bigger than all of us.

TITLE: "My Home Town"
AUTHOR: Mary Gentry
AGE: 624
OCCUPATION: ?

This entry is a bit late in coming, so I hope you'll forgive that. I tend to lose track of time. But tonight has been so quiet—not a cricket, dog bark or hoot of owl—that it almost seemed time had paused in its eternal flight. Which caused *me* to pause. And to remember the radio contest.

For all the years behind me I still enjoy and cherish brevity in some things, so I will not write at length.

This town, *my* town, has been home for a long, long time. Longer than any of my other homes. I care for it and about it, although it isn't always easy and my patience is often sorely tested.

But what most impresses me about Uncanny Valley is its *endurance*: something to which I can relate with much experience.

It changes on the outside yet somehow remains the same.

It balances its humours, even on dark days.

It exhibits tenaciousness, although often all but forgotten except by itself.

Uncanny Valley does all these things.

Dare I predict that somehow it always will?

Utterly charming. And very much Home.

There, now. A fine orange sunset to write by, although it seems a bit early this evening.

And now I am done.

Epilogue

In the months following the end of the essay contest, a number of WRDB employees undertook independent research in order to shed light on the circumstances of the Uncanny submissions. Below are the limited findings. The most likely explanation is, as already stated, that someone carried out an elaborate hoax for reasons unknown. However, the question of authenticity is not the focus of the following findings, which ultimately provide just as many questions as answers. That will have to wait for later, more extensive investigation.

1) *Internet search engines turn up very few references to a town in Western Pennsylvania called "Uncanny Valley." (A "Google" search, for instance, brings up thousands of references to Masahiro Mori's theory of "Uncanny Valley" as it pertains to robotics, but only one or two passing references to the town.)*

2) *Several elderly sources in the small Western Pennsylvania towns of Dayton, Sagamore, and Plumville confirm the existence of Uncanny Valley, along with its complete destruction from suspected arson...<u>sixty-two years ago</u>.*

3) *Those same sources are surprisingly reticent to talk about the town or its fate, a typical response being, "Some things are best left forgotten," or, "Beyond that, there's not much else to say."*

4) *All sources make the (highly unlikely) claim that they can't remember exactly where the town once was, one*

stating that, "It's probably all woods now, and I doubt even a dirt road goes through there no more." Maps from the 1940s and before don't show it. Census listings don't include it.

5) *Several historical societies from the above-mentioned towns, as well as the towns of Rural Valley, Kittaning, and NuMine, possess bound or microfilmed archives of local newspapers. Those from mid to late-1948 confirm a massive town-wide fire on the evening of June 8th that resulted in <u>one hundred and ninety-two deaths</u>. If accurate, this suggests a tragedy of national significance, which makes the lack of published information on any scale all the more extraordinary.*

6) *Follow-up data on burials, memorials, charitable fundraising efforts for survivors, etc., is non-existent. It is almost as if, following the tragedy, Uncanny Valley simply disappeared from the awareness of a public that rarely thought of it to begin with.*

7) *A Dayton historian named Emil Fitzhugh claims the town "left a bad taste in people's mouths" and that the land where it used to be is now "shunned by those who remember it." He claims to have been to the ruins twice, once in 1954 and again in 1978. "Never again," he said. When asked why, he simply responded, "I saw things I wish I hadn't."*

There is little more to relate, except that the envelopes of each submission were mailed with three-cent stamps, and postmarked between March 21 and June 9, 1948.

*****

One final, late finding:
Three days ago WRDB received a photocopied list of the Uncanny Valley fire victims from the Rural Valley Historical Society. Twenty-seven of the essay authors have names that match those of people who perished in the blaze.

--Gregory Miller
July 14, 2010
Pittsburgh, PA

Acknowledgments

These stories were first published in the following venues, and are reprinted with permission:

"The White Dove" in *Wretched Moments*. Pill Hill Press, 2010.

"In Tune" in *Darkest Secrets*. Static Movement, 2010.

"The Fourth Floor" in *The Shadow People*. Static Movement, 2011.

"My Flower" in *Howl: Tales of the Feral and Infernal*. Lame Goat Press, 2010.

"Mittens' Last Catch" in *Pot Luck: Flash Fiction*. Static Movement, 2011.

"Keeping Dry" in *Unquiet Earth: An Anthology of Zombie Flash*. Static Movement, 2011.

"Here and There" in *Oh, the Horror*. Static Movement, 2010.

"Out of the Blue" in *Daily Flash: 365 Days of Flash Fiction*. Pill Hill Press, 2010.

"What Happened to Charlie" in *Pot Luck: Flash Fiction*. Static Movement, 2011.

"Best Kept Secret" in *Faeries*. Static Movement, 2010.

"My Gift" in *Christmas Fear*. Static Movement, 2010.

"The Good Job" in *Inner Fears*. Static Movement, 2010.

"My Ghost" in *Something Dark in the Doorway*. Static Movement, 2010.

"The Bad Spot" in *Novus Creatura*. Sam's Dot Publishing, 2010.

"Ms. Jennings' Family" in *Madness of the Mind*. Static Movement, 2010.

"Nihil Obstat" in *Their Dark Masters*. Red Skies Press, 2011.

"The Sounding of the Sea" in *The Sounding of the Sea: Five Tales of Loss and Redemption*. Lame Goat Press, 2010.

"I Got a Secret" in *School Days*. Static Movement, 2010.

All other stories are original to this collection.

About the Author

Gregory Miller was born in State College, Pennsylvania in 1978. His short stories, poetry, and essays have appeared in over 60 publications. In addition to *The Uncanny Valley: Tales from a Lost Town*, he is also the author of *Crows at Twilight*, an omnibus edition of the 43 stories that comprised his first two collections. A high school English teacher for over a decade, he lives in Pittsburgh with his family, where he is currently working on a prequel to *The Uncanny Valley*. Miller's website/blog is:

http://author gregorymiller.wordpress.com/

About the Illustrator

John Randall York was born in Tyler, Texas and grew up playing and working in a small zoo where his father was the director. He loves ghost stories, old horror movies, and illustrations from the middle 20th century. He also enjoys writing songs and playing guitar.

In addition to *The Uncanny Valley*, John has illustrated *Scaring the Crows: 21 Tales for Noon or Midnight, On the Edge of Twilight: 22 Tales to Follow You Home, Crows at Twilight: An Omnibus of Tales*, and the cover of *The Sounding of the Sea: Five Tales of Loss and Redemption*, all by Gregory Miller. He also recently wrote and illustrated his first children's book, *King Bronty*, published by StoneGarden.net.

He currently lives in Tyler, Texas with his wife and three cats.

CPSIA information can be obtained
at www.ICGtesting.com
Printed in the USA
BVHW040220150321
602541BV00028B/552

9 781494 852870